Kenton

THE MCCADE DRAGON BOOK 1

KATHI S. BARTON

World Castle Publishing, LLC
Pensacola, Florida
Copyright © Kathi S. Barton 2016
Paperback ISBN: 9781629894386
eBook ISBN: 9781629894393
First Edition World Castle Publishing, LLC, March 7, 2016
http://www.worldcastlepublishing.com
Licensing Notes
Cover: Karen Fuller
Editor: Eric Johnston
Editor: Maxine Bringenberg

Chapter 1

"I need you to tell me what this is worth." Emma looked up at the man that held out a little box to her. If it was in her power, Emma would gladly have punched him in the nose. But she also knew that he'd hit her back, and it would be ten times more painful than anything she could do to him. "Now, Emma. And he said for you not to dally. He needs it now."

"So, you do it. I'm in the middle of something else you told me to do." She knew as well as he did that Bart could tell the worth of an item almost as well as she could. Not quite as good as she could; practice had made her better and faster at it. But they'd both been trained to know how to do it. "I'm in the middle of—"

She should have known better. Whenever she pointed something obvious out to her brother, he would resort to violence if he didn't care for her answer. Which was usually all the time. Emma wondered if she'd ever learn and doubted it. Now she found herself on the floor with her mouth bloodied and her head hurting. Not the first time for that either.

He put the box on the desk, then pulled out his gun and laid it on her desk with it as if that was all he needed to make her comply. The punch to her face had done that pretty good, she thought. Emma wished she could pick the gun up and blow his fucking head off. Instead, she lifted her hurting body up and got back to her desk. Emma didn't even bother wiping the blood off. He'd just hit her again to show he could.

Picking up the small box, she opened it. Inside was a small blue bag, tied at the top with an equally blue string. There were no markings on the bag or the box, but she knew quality when she felt it. And this bag wasn't it. She started to ask Bart what kind of joke this was when she realized that he'd not answer her. He'd more than likely do what she'd wanted to do to him and shoot her. She'd be dead and he'd be standing over her demanding that she get up and do what he'd told her to do. There was no love lost between the two of them, and hadn't been for a very long time.

Dumping the contents out into her hand, she was first surprised at the weight of the ring, then at how big it was. But the ring itself was what had her holding her breath. It was simply the most beautiful thing she'd ever seen. The work on it—and there was a great deal of it—had been done with a steady hand and an even better eye, for the art looked to her like the person who had made this loved the person who was to receive it. For a second she wondered if she would ever have someone love her that much. She looked up at Bart when he snorted at her. He looked pissed.

"It's just a band. Nothing but a damned gold band that is worth less than my fucking shoes. I wonder if it's even gold plated. Fuckers." She looked at the ring, then back at him as he continued. "Fucking bastard said it was worth millions. It's not even worth the box it came in. Why the hell do I even bother with robbing people if they're going to lie to me about what I'm taking? Huh? And then to have fought so hard to keep it? As if it was worth his own life? Dumbass probably believed that it was worth the money I was told it was."

"Are you kidding me? This isn't just a band, dumbass. This is a work of art." She started to show him, but Bart picked up his gun and slid it back into his holster before slamming his hands down on the table, his face level with her. She leapt back from him. Which, she supposed, was what he had wanted her to do anyway. Then he laughed at her. "Don't hurt me, Bart. Please? I'll tell Daddy."

"Like he gives a shit about you. I mean, look where he has you working. In the basement of a piece of shit building that has nothing to go for it but a toilet that is ten feet away." He snorted again. "Go to him, Emma, see if I'm not right. And when he tells you to go away, I'm going to come back down here and blow your fucking brains out for bothering him. We have more important things to do than to listen to you whine about how badly you're being treated."

After he left her, she put the ring back in the little bag and started working on the chains that had been tangled up when Bart had simply tossed them into a bank bag. He'd told her when she asked him that it wasn't his job to make sure that things were neat and tidy, that she would be out of a fucking job if he did. She estimated that she had about ten hours in untangling the chains so far and she wasn't any closer to getting them straight than she had been before. Emma was pretty sure that he'd done it on purpose. It was something he loved doing, making her job more difficult.

Her father and brother had dumped her down here six years ago, pulling her from college and telling her that she had to earn her keep. Of course Emma hadn't seen her father in all this time. Words, harsh and mean, had come from him via her brother. She was going to have to find another job soon. This one just wasn't making it for her any longer. Of course, she blamed that on Bart too. He took money from her cash envelope every week, and he was taking more and more all the time. He called it a living tax. If he didn't get it, she didn't live. And she believed him too.

The ring called to her. She knew that was silly. Rings or other things didn't talk, but she could almost hear it telling her that it didn't belong to her and that she needed to return it to the owner. She would love to do that, but she wasn't going to. Not that she'd have the chance to get out of this place with the thing. Being patted down and wanded every time she left would have made it impossible, but she knew that if found out, she'd be dead. Emma looked over at the desk next to hers.

Sebastian Logan had been her friend and co-worker, and the nicest man she'd ever known. Polite, hardworking, and a man who had loved his family more than he did his own life. And it was what had gotten him killed.

A diamond ring had been brought in a month ago. Bart, of course, had deemed it unworthy and had told her and Sebastian they could have it. She'd thought it was pretty but thought that Sebastian could sell it for a few dollars, and knew that it would help out in their situation. His only child was sick and that money would have gone a long way in helping him. So he'd taken the ring home to sell.

He'd come in the next day, saying that he'd gotten enough to buy a prescription that was much needed, and they had both sat down to work. An hour later, Bart and his friend, Mark Whitaker, had come in to question Sebastian about it. Apparently a fence that they knew had mentioned that Sebastian had brought it in.

"You said I could have it. You told us it was worthless and that we could have it. Tell him, Emma. Tell him he said that." Bart, of course, denied that, and even told Emma that their father wanted to make an example of Sebastian. Bart had pulled his gun free and had killed her friend right there in front of her, despite her begging him to let it go.

Blood had sprayed over her face and clothing. Bart had set Mark in front of her for the rest of the day while Sebastian was lying in his own blood, and told her that if she wiped her face he would put the blood back. But this time it would be her own.

All Emma wanted to do was get out of there and be her own person. Live her life as she wanted on her own terms. As soon as she could save enough money to get away, anyway. Looking at the ring again, she wondered what would happen if she were to get it to its owner. What sort of reward would there be? Because at the rate she was saving money, she'd be too old to run when she did manage to get enough to go on.

At ten after twelve, she pulled out her lunch. It was only a jelly sandwich; the peanut butter had run out a few days ago. Emma wanted to cry about what her life had become, and knew that it was as set in stone as the sword was that she'd read about so long ago.

"Put that shit away. I want you to look this over." She only glanced at the paperwork that Bart had tossed in front of her. Her lunch time was her time, not his. She'd told him that before. Not that it mattered, but she had told him. "Now, Emma. I want to get it to Dad before the end of the day, and you fucking around is gonna make me late."

"I'm eating. And in the event that you missed that part, I'm entitled to have one hour for my lunch. So come back when I'm done." He drew his fist back and she tilted out her chin. "Hit me, and see if I don't go home because of it. Go ahead, Bart, knock me around and you'll never get this."

"He wants it now." Emma took a bite of her sandwich and said nothing. "You fucking cunt. You think this is going to win you any points with me? Who do you think is going to run this place when Dad finally kicks the bucket? You? Not fucking likely."

He slammed his fists on the table again, a thing he did when he wasn't winning an argument. Well, she'd had a shitty day so far, and right now she really did want him to hit her. She would go to her father this time.

Sweeping everything off her desk in his fit of anger, he stood over her, watching. Emma reached for the little box and the ring that had fallen out of it by bending over and leaning under her desk. Just at that moment an explosion rocked the room. There wasn't time to think, not even to wonder what Bart had done now.

Emma felt it singe her arms and legs even as the ring slipped over the tip of her finger. She and the desk went flying back; she felt it hit her several times as heat poured into the room with her. Screams filled the air...not just hers, but her brother's as well. Then everything went black.

Wake up. She felt rather than heard someone telling her to wake. The pain over her body told her that she'd be better off just letting things fade out again, but the voice in her head...it felt like it told her again to wake up.

"I hurt." The voice, calmer now, told her that she'd be better if she got up and moved. "I don't think so. I think I'm broken."

You are not broken. Not too badly, that is. Come on now, get out of this place before the others come to find you. She had no idea why that would be a bad thing when the voice spoke again. *Should they find you, then all will be lost. Come on now, Emma, you must get moving. Moving will be good for us both. No one must find you here with me.*

"Both? Who is here with me? Hello?" No answer. But then she thought there shouldn't be because as far as she knew, there was only one of her. Giggling hurt a little, so she tried to tell herself that she really did need to move.

Every time she moved something off her, there seemed to be tons more atop her. Wood and bricks. Glass surrounded her, and it seemed to be in her as well. The desk, she knew, had more than likely saved her life. Had she been sitting at it instead of nearly under it, she would have been killed. She did pause a moment to wonder if Bart had made it, but found that she really didn't care. Bart was on his own for now.

The debris was thick around her too. Papers were everywhere, most of them still smoldering. The chair that she'd been in was a broken mess imbedded in the wall above her head.

Once she cleared herself of what she could to move, Emma could see the street beyond. Whatever had blown up had taken out the five floors above her sublevel work station. Gingerly, she made her way to the opening, only to be stopped by the voice again

No, no, not that way. Go to the back of the ruin. I'll guide you. She turned then, not even sure why she was listening to the voice instead of common sense, but she was hurting too badly to argue with herself right now. There were people out there in front of her. She had no idea what she'd find behind her. But she made her way out the way the voice told her.

It seemed to take her too long to get out. Falling twice, she bumped her head again and had to lay there for a long time to let the dizziness stop. Emma was sick too, her belly not liking the way her vision kept going in and out all the time. And she knew that the long gash in her leg wasn't good. The blood pouring from it was thick with dirt.

As soon as she was out of the building, she lay back against the one across from it and looked at where she'd been. There was no way she should have survived that, and she was sure that anyone else in the building hadn't. Emma wondered who besides her brother and her were there, if anyone. And again, she wondered how the hell she had survived.

The building had been one of the oldest downtown. At five stories, it had once been the home to a textile company that had gone under in the twenties. Her father had acquired the building, along with several more, a few years ago, and had taken this one to use as an office of sorts. It was a front, like most of her father's businesses, Bart had told her.

Emma didn't know. Her brother never put her dad in the best picture when he talked about him. He was ruthless, a murderer, and even a thug when necessary. If he was as Bart said, he had changed a great deal since her mother had died a few years back.

The building now looked like it had never been there. A deep hole—a crater, she figured it would be called—was where it had once been. Nothing had survived on either side of it either. The two buildings that were used as storage units for whatever her father had acquired were leveled. Even the one across from the building had suffered some major damage. Emma watched as the first firetruck pulled up in front of the mess.

Your father is dead, I'm afraid. She nodded at the voice, then regretted that immediately. *Your brother is alive, but he is badly burned. He and another man, his bodyguard, will be pulled from the wreckage soon, but they will not mention you are here. But they will come for you now. The others will come.*

"Who will? Why?" The voice told her that it was because of him. "Him who? I don't know anyone. I don't date, I'm not allowed. I don't even know why I have this voice talking to me. Do you? Am I…I don't know, am I dead too?"

You are not dead, Emma, but they come for me. And the rest of us now that I'm awake. There will be more coming now that I've been found. She stood up then, determined to go and see if someone could patch her up. *You do and they'll kill you where you stand.*

"Why? What did I do? This was…it was more than likely a gas explosion." The voice told her she knew better. "No, I don't. I don't know a damned thing. For all I know, I could be lying there dead in that thing and this is all a dream."

I'm not a dream, Emma Gentry. I am part of the dragon in the ring. Emma stopped moving and looked down at her hand. There it was, the ring. Just on the tip of her finger. *When you slipped it upon your finger, I knew then that you were the one to carry me. The one that would take me to my owner. You will, won't you? Take me home to the one that awaits me? The rest of me will follow now that I have found you.*

"No. In the event you didn't notice, I'm out of work, no money, and I don't even know what is wrong with me that I can hear you talking to me. I'm hurting, injured, and you won't let me go and find someone to fix me up." He told her that she was the one, and that he would see that she had such riches if she did this for him. "The one what? I'm just a woman trying to get along in this world my family brought me into. Can't you just leave me alone? Please?"

I can keep you safe. And if you promise to take me to my owner, I will help you in ways that you will need. I will, as I have said, make you a queen that will never have to worry for money again. I am but a part of the whole. A dragon that must be brought together with the other pieces of my set. Emma just wanted to take a nap. Forever. *No, you will need to keep moving. The man that your brother stole me from, he will come for you because of the ring. He will want you dead because of the ring.*

"Why?" He didn't answer her and she realized that she'd been asking that a lot to the unknown. "Fine. I'm going to do this for you, but you're going to have to do something for me. I want you to not do a damned thing for me unless it's to guide me. I know better than most that nothing in this world comes without consequences. So tell me where to go and nothing else."

Nothing? She told him again that she didn't want to owe him anything when this was done. *All right. But I think that you will come to regret that soon enough.*

She already did. Moving in the direction that he told her, she felt like she'd broken more bones than she knew she had. While he told her that she needed to go north, Emma told him that she needed to go to her home. There she'd get cleaned up and retrieve the last of her funds. She had no idea where she was going, but wherever it was, it wasn't going to be a free ride. Emma thought that whoever was coming for her would think she was dead long enough for her to get out of her apartment to rid herself of the voice.

Emma knew on some level that the voice was her own. There simply wasn't any way for her to be talking to the dragon of the ring. She wanted out and this was her subconscious getting her there. So what if the world thought her dead? She was fine with that as well. Emma Gentry was dead as far as she was concerned too, and she'd have to come up with a name that would work. As she showered and changed, cleaning up as much of the wounds on her body that she could, Emma thought of what her life would be now.

"Anything I want." She smiled at herself and winced. The cuts on her face made even doing the simplest things hard. She did worry over the wound in her leg, but at least it was clean, and the bleeding had stopped as well…for now. As she moved out of her home, she looked around. There was nothing there, not one thing she would miss. This Emma was dead.

~~~

"Twenty-four dead and several dozen more injured in the blast that is still under investigation. There was some talk of gas leaks, but that was ruled out when it was said that the building called Shipley Textile was the epicenter of the explosion, and there were no gas lines to that building."

Baldwin Franks wanted to throw something at the television but refrained. He was a man that prided himself on control. But the newsperson was not giving him the answers that he craved. He wanted to know if Bartholomew Gentry and his son had survived, not the dozens of nameless fucks that meant nothing to him. When the news anchor paused, pushing her finger to her ear, he wanted to scream at her that no one believed that she was listening to a fucking thing, but then she turned to the scene behind her.

"There is news just in that Mr. Bart Gentry, Junior has been pulled from the wreckage, along with another man by the name of Whitaker. That is all that we know right now. Mr. Gentry is the son of Bartholomew Gentry, Senior, a man who owned a great many of the buildings in the downtown area. Mr. Gentry and his son have been under a great deal of scrutiny for the last several years, starting with the death of the senior Mr. Gentry's wife, Anderson Franks Gentry, some years ago. Mr. Gentry, Senior's body, along with five more, was pulled from the building about an hour ago, I'm told."

Baldwin leaned back in his chair as the anchor continued about the things she had little to no real information about. Gentry Senior was dead. Baldwin thought that they both should have been dead, but was sure that the man who'd survived, a man he'd come to hate more than anything, would land on his feet. Or in this case, flat on his back. The sooner the entire family was dead, the happier he'd be. They'd killed his little girl.

He looked over at his man, Steward Jefferies, and told him to get someone on it. Steward's phone rang before he could answer Baldwin.

As the other man listened to his call, Baldwin thought of all the ways he'd wanted to make both Gentry men suffer. There had been times when he'd had Bart in his sights, but something would always come up. This time he knew he'd taken drastic measures, but the man was just where he wanted him. It was way past time to kill Bart, and he was going to be the one to do it, even if he had to do it in front of a bunch of cops.

When Steward hung up, he looked pale as he leaned back in his chair. Baldwin was almost afraid to ask him what it was, but wasn't going to seem as if he cared. He not only was in control of things around him, he also never gave the appearance of caring much about it.

16

"Apparently Emma Gentry isn't dead, as we'd been told, and was in the building when it blew." Baldwin nearly screamed out his frustrations. Would this family never fucking end? "So far they've not found a trace of her in the number of dead, and she's not on the injury list, either, that they can find. I don't...someone saw her climbing out of the sublevel of the basement just as the police arrived. I have a man on it."

"How do you know it was my granddaughter and not some rat climbing out of her hole after a night of fucking whatever had a dick?" Steward stood up and went to his briefcase. Pulling out the file that was on top, he handed it to him. "What is this?"

"I told you several days ago that there was rumor that Emma was alive and hiding out somewhere. We could never confirm nor deny that information, so you told me to keep on it. I had someone follow her and she lives...lived in a poor neighborhood that catered more to the people that her father worked with than his type of wealth. There wasn't any reason to believe that she was this person, due to her living conditions, and I nearly tossed it away as just that, rumors. But then we got a picture of her just this morning. I forgot until just this minute that I had it." Baldwin looked at the picture and felt his heart twist up in his chest. "They have some of her DNA that I'm running, but so far I've not heard back. But the girl in this picture looks like your daughter Anderson, doesn't she? I don't know why she's been hiding out the way she has, but I intend to find out."

"Yes." Baldwin looked at the blurred picture of the woman. Even with the poor quality of the picture, he knew that it was her. "Call them up, rush it. I want to know now."

He looked at Steward when he said nothing. There was more, he just knew it, and when he got the information, his well-controlled temper was going to detonate. He told him to tell him.

"The ring was in the building." The fucking ring. The motherfucking ring was there and not where it was supposed to be. Which was with him. "Bart, the younger, took it from the courier this morning. Killed him and three other men while they were en route to us. He took not just the ring, which was the most valuable piece, but he also took the money they were bringing here. I'm guessing that it, as well as the cash, was in the building when it went up. I'm going to have his home searched, of course, but I'd not hold out much hope. The kid, for all his stupidity, seemed to know just when to lay low."

"Why wasn't I told about this before now?" Steward told him that he'd only just found out too. "And how do we know that it's him? And not some random fuck that is going to die too?"

"He left you a note. Well, not you, but the person he was robbing." Baldwin asked him what it said. "It says thank you for the money, that he really did appreciate it, and that when you sent some more this way for him, to make sure that you made the pick-up easier, as in boxes and not suitcases."

Baldwin was happy to know that Bart had no idea what he'd found in the ring. Few ever would, and when he had all the pieces, he'd be the wealthiest and the strongest man in the world. He had only to find all six pieces to make that happen.

The legend, one as old as the earth, had fallen in his lap some time ago and he'd been searching for the pieces since. He and two other people, enemies of his, were the only ones that had an inkling as to what the jewels were really for.

"Kill him." Steward nodded and asked about the girl. "Her too. If she is Gentry's daughter, then she's just as guilty for killing my daughter as the rest of them." No witnesses were the only way to ensure that he got what he wanted in this.

It hurt him to say that, almost as much as it had when he'd been told that his lovely little girl, Anderson, had been killed when they'd thought she was her husband in the car. But the entire family needed to be purged from the earth, and if he had to murder his own flesh and blood to do so, then he would. When Steward left him, Baldwin picked up the picture again and looked at it. It was as if he were looking at his little girl again before she'd been pulled into the life of crime with her husband.

Anderson had been…well, willful didn't begin to cover what his little girl had been. She had a mind of her own, and damn the person that had any other opinion than hers. Even he had butted heads with her from time to time, and had, in the end, decided that it was easier to give in than to fight with her. That was how she'd ended up married to his worst enemy. Bartholomew had been a thorn in his side then, and had been placed on his list of ones who needed to die when his daughter had called him from the accident she'd been in that night so long ago.

"Someone hit me. I think…I'm hurt badly." He asked her who'd done it, his mind not fully awake when the call had come to his home in the middle of the night. "Bartholomew. Help me. I don't know yet what's going on, but I don't want to die."

Baldwin could hear the sirens then, the men coming to rescue his little girl, knowing that it was going to be too late for her. She told him that she was sorry that she couldn't hang on for him. Then the line had gone dead; his little girl was gone from him forever.

Chapter 2

"Doctor McCade, there are two more patients to see you if you have time." He looked at his nurse and wanted to sob. He'd been working since four this morning and it never seemed to end. "One of them is the Mason boy. He's *fallen* again."

Fallen. Of course he had. And his father wasn't beating the shit out of him to make him fall. Kenton told her to put young Jim in the room, and then told her to call child services. It was well past time to do something.

"Tell them to come to the back. We'll scoop him out that way. Who is he with this time? Grandma or just him?" She told him Grandma was sitting with the child, Dad was in the car. "Good. Tell her that we're done and then show her to the other room. Is she hurt too?"

"Black eye. I think she'll about go with anything you want this time. I think she's had enough too." Kenton nodded. Some people did not deserve what was given to them. "What about the father? He's here too this time, but not in the building as yet. Grandma is holding onto the kid like he's her lifeline."

"I'm sure she knows that I've had about enough. And taking Jim to the hospital would have gotten the dad arrested this time." Kenton stood up and stretched, feeling his animal move along with him. "Move them around, leave the rest to me."

Kenton knew that this was going to end badly. He actually hoped that it would. He was tired, his head hurt, and he wanted to go home. Calling out to his brother Jorden, he asked him to come to his office. He knew that he was working on a piece of art and would come if he asked. His brother shared a building with him but not a practice. Jorden was an artist, and used the lower part of the building for his studio. Also the upper level when the mood stuck him.

Jim Mason has been hurt again. Can you come here? Give me a little help in the event I have to murder his father?

Why don't you just do it and do the world a favor? The bastard has been hurting that kid since the day he was born. Just let go and take care of him. He could hear the humor in his brother's voice, but was pretty sure that he was partly serious as well. *Where is the fucking shit? Your office again?*

Yes. He and his mother-in-law are here with him. I'm having Cortland put Jim in one office, the grandmother in another. She's been beaten too, I think. Jorden said he was on his way. *I've called Children's Services this time as well.*

Good. I'm just outside your offices. Let me see what is up before you come out. He told him to go ahead. *Yes, the kid is hurting. Badly too, if his face is any indication. Also, I think Grandma might have more than a black eye. She's not breathing all that well. Do you suppose he has been hurting her all this time too?*

More than likely. He's a fucking bully and taking it out on someone much smaller than him. I will be happy when this is done. Maybe he'll find him a nice friend in prison that will show him what it feels like to have the shit knocked out of him all the time.

Kenton moved to the hallway to see where Cortland was taking his patients. He listened as his brother spoke to her in the hallway just outside of his waiting room, and then to Mr. Mason. Apparently the man was not happy with the turn of events. He thought he should stay with his boy.

"Mr. Mason, you know that you can't do that. I've told you before that Doctor McCade likes to talk to his patients alone for a few minutes." There were some mumbled words, and Kenton walked into the waiting room just as Mason stood up. The man puffed out his chest, but Kenton was still much bigger.

"You think you can just order me to wait out here while you put stuff in his head?" Kenton asked him what sort of things he could put into his son's head. "You know what shit I'm talking about. How do I know you don't tell him that you wanna have sex with him or some shit?"

Kenton looked at young Jim. "You go on back with Cortland, Jim, and I'll have a talk with your father." Jim looked scared, which Kenton was pretty sure he was. But after reassuring him things would be all right, Jim went with his grandmother and Cortland. Kenton turned to the piece of shit in front of him.

"You aren't getting him back this time." Mason— Kenton wasn't sure what his first name was—lunged at him, and Kenton shoved him back into the seat he'd been occupying. Leaning over the fat man, he put his face right next to his and smiled. "Try it and they'll be taking you out of here in a body bag and not on a stretcher. I'm in a foul mood, and would love to make sure that Jim and his grandmother are safe."

"You think you know it all, don't you? You fucking bastard. I want him back out here now. You hear me? If you don't, then I'm gonna say you kidnapped him from me. And you can bet that I don't think we're going to be needing your services no more. You're gonna hear from my attorney too." Kenton asked him if he could afford that. "You don't got no business asking me what I can and can't afford. I know my rights."

"Yes, I'm sure you do. But I know the rights of the two people in the other rooms." When Mason lunged at him again, Kenton let him. He knew that it was going to hurt, but he also knew that whatever the pain, it would be worth it. He just didn't expect the knife that was stuck in his belly when he hit him.

As he fell back, he saw Jorden hit Mason. Whether or not he killed him was beyond Kenton's control right now. He was bleeding and hurting, and the man had done it. Looking up at the person that said his name, he wondered for a second when Jorden had changed. Then he realized it was a cop.

"Doctor McCade? Can you hear me?" It was on the tip of Kenton's tongue to tell him he'd been stabbed in the belly, not the ear when the man continued. "We've called for an ambulance for you. And the other two as well. We got Mason in custody."

"Good. I think he tried to kill me." The cop said that was sure enough. "My brother, where is he?"

"He's calling your momma. I don't think she's going to be none too happy with you either." No, she'd be pissed was what she'd be. He'd promised her that he'd be safe working at his own practice and not the hospital emergency room where he'd been working before. "We're taking you in now."

He tried to tell him that Jim needed to be helped first, but he saw Jorden then. He looked grim. Kenton asked him what had happened. He didn't think he was going to like that answer either.

"Mom is on her way. She said you'd better not die or she's going to be very disappointed in you." Kenton told his brother he would be as well. "Yeah, well I'd work real hard at not pissing Mom off any more if I were you. She's pretty upset that you lied to her."

Kenton said nothing. He was working hard on not screaming like a baby. He looked down at the knife that was still protruding from his belly and asked why he was still wearing it. Jorden laughed.

"Because we told him not to remove it. We don't know what it might be touching or cutting into." Kenton looked at the man standing over him and told his friend and former colleague, Walker, hi. "Don't *hi* me, you moron. You're supposed to come to my wedding on Saturday, not be laid up in the hospital with a knife wound that you could have easily avoided."

"Yeah, but then I'd not get the prick who did this to me in jail." Walker growled at him but said nothing more. "He hit his kid, Walker. That's the carnal sin of fatherhood."

"So stabbing you is okay?" Kenton said that it wasn't, but it was better than him stabbing someone else. "I know that. But you are still losing blood like it's your business. And I'm not tangling with your mom. She's fucking scary."

She was also the most loving person he knew. As he was told to breathe deeply, Kenton thought of his poor mom. She really was going to be upset with him. He'd broken his promise to be safe. His dragon was afraid of her too, Kenton thought when his beast moved along his body.

As he faded out, whatever they were giving him kicking in, he wondered what was going to happen now. The kid would be safe for a while; the grandmother too. He looked at Jorden when he suddenly appeared in front of him.

"Hide them." Jorden nodded. "Give them whatever it takes to get them both to safety. We both know that he won't be stopped this time."

"I'll take care of it." Kenton closed his eyes and let the drugs kick his ass. He knew that Jorden would do what he asked and that Jim and his grandma would be okay no matter what.

~~~

Emma knew that if she didn't get some rest soon, she'd be dead. The dragon in her head told her again that she needed to break into the building she was standing in front of. But for the life of her all she could think about was the last time she'd eaten more than a few bites and when she hadn't hurt like she'd been run over. It had been over two weeks since she'd been tossed around in her father's building, and she knew she wasn't getting any better. The wound in her leg was giving her the worst kind of pain, and she was sure that it was infected.

There are things in this building that can help you. I know that you told me not to help you this way, but you are losing ground daily and they'll catch you soon. She wanted to tell him to shut up, that she knew that, but it took too much effort to argue with him again. *Emma, you need to do as I have said. If you die, all will be lost.*

"Why don't you do it? I mean, you're a dragon and all, or so you tell me. I'm sure that you're considerably bigger than me. You break in, get what I need, and come back here and fix me." He told her that he didn't work that way. "Of course not. You're this all-powerful being and until you get to your owner, you're just a ring. While I, on the other hand, am sick, hungry, and in pain."

I'm only partly here in the ring. I am not the ring. You will understand when you return me to my owner. My owner will know what I'm about. There are more of us too, as I have said. Once we are all together again, we will be powerful. Emma had heard that before too. How there wasn't just the ring but an entire set of shit that this dragon was stuck in. At this point, she just didn't care anymore.

She moved to the door again, the one at the back of the building, and shoved her weak body against it. She was surprised when it gave, like she'd really done some damage to it. Then Emma saw that it wasn't locked. The turnkey that held it locked at been left undone. Moving into the building, she was surprised to find it was some sort of office, a series of offices.

A doctor works here and an artist, I think. I can smell paints and canvas. Also clay. A beautiful medium, clay. She asked the dragon if he was going to help her. *No. I know not where he is now, but this is his office. Here is where you can get what you need to repair yourself.*

"How do you know this crap?" He, of course, didn't answer her. Whenever she asked him something that he didn't want her to know, he'd just not answer. Of course it would be hard for him to know most of the things she didn't since she didn't know the answers either. The thing was a figment of her fevered mind.

Emma moved to where she thought that some drugs might be. She didn't want to steal them, or even sell them, though the money would be good right now. She just wanted something to take the pain away. And maybe fix up her ribs. Then when that didn't hurt as much, she'd try to stitch up her leg, maybe clean it up again.

The dragon—or whatever he was—had told her that she had several broken ribs, her arm was badly sprained, and she had several lacerations on her body that would need stitches. But he, too, was worried about the long gash in her leg. It was puffy and red. She couldn't go to a hospital, she knew that now, nor could she see any kind of doctor that might turn her into the police. Or whoever was out for her. She'd been shot at twice since she'd crawled out of the building. She was sure that the next time she'd be dead.

The offices were clean and smelled fresh, something that she'd missed since she'd started this haphazard trip. Most of the time she slept in alleys, with nothing more than a pile of smelly clothing as her blanket. And food was as hard to come by as places to rest. Twice she'd been able to go into a building, and both times she'd been caught there. Had the "dragon" not helped her out, she was sure that whoever was chasing her would have cornered her and killed her.

"How do they find me? You never said." He asked her who. "The bastards that keep shooting at me. And don't think I didn't notice that you didn't answer me about why I can't take this ring off and leave it someplace."

They find you because they know you. That made even less sense than when he'd told her that if she died, he would too. Well, duh, she wanted to tell him. They were the same person. *They have people everywhere looking for you. They know who you are and your face. But they know not that you have me. Not as yet.*

That was another thing. He never told her who was looking for her. Not that she knew either, but it would help to know what sort of enemy she'd made that would hunt her down as this person was. And for what reason? A ring? Not likely. It was more than likely some enemy of her brother or her dad.

She found a room that was filled with all kinds of medical supplies. She pulled gauze and tape off the shelves, and she found a few dozen bottles of pills still on the shelf. But she left them alone. She wasn't a doctor so had no idea what they were used for. But the rest she could use.

Sitting on the floor, she pulled the dirty rag that she'd found a few days ago off her leg. Dark pus was seeping from the wound now, and it smelled badly. It would be her luck that she'd die from an infection rather than being shot, which she was sure would be much quicker.

Pouring an entire bottle of peroxide over the wound, she watched it bubble up and drain off her leg. It burned, but it also felt cool against her skin. Then when she took a small piece of gauze and rubbed over it, she could see that it was much worse than she'd first thought. The wound was seeping green goo now, and no longer bleeding.

Getting up, dizzy again, she held onto the table until she thought she could move without falling. When she was ready, she moved back to the shelves and found several more bottles of peroxide, as well as something to clean up with when she was done. Emma thought if she could clean this up, she might just make it to the owner of the ring. Sitting down, Emma had to close her eyes just for a moment before beginning again.

You are unwell. Emma didn't bother answering. *You will need help if you are to return me to my owner. You must not get sicker, Emma. You will need someone to help you if you are to survive this.*

"Yeah, well, you said that if I went to the hospital, they'd find me and kill everyone that helped me. You told me if I went to my doctor, should I have been able to afford it, they'd find me. And kill him too." She laughed a little, not really finding any humor in this all. "It's not really a win-win situation for me, do you think? I mean, death by gunshot or death by infection."

"Do you always talk to yourself when you break and enter?" It took her several seconds to realize it wasn't the dragon speaking, and opened her eyes to stare at the man standing in the doorway. "I can smell the infection from here. Are you planning to die here or did you come here for help?"

"Both?" The man nodded and moved into the room with her. "I can't let you help me. He said it would get you killed. I don't know why I believe him, but it could be because I've been shot at twice in the last few weeks. But if you could just tell me which one of those drugs will take the pain away, I'd be really appreciative of it. I hurt like hell."

"I bet you do. But I'm not going to call for help, if that's what you're saying. I don't know why, but I have a feeling you will never make it to the hospital. How long have you been like this?" She told him that she had no idea really any more. Then she heard him hiss when he pulled the gauze away that she'd just put over the cut in her leg. "You're going to need some serious help. Are you sure you don't know how long have you been running?"

"I really don't know. Forever, I think. I hurt too." He lifted her up in his arms and put her on the table she'd been leaning against earlier. "I have to find this person to give them this ring. Do you think you can fix me up so I can do that?"

"I'm not a doctor. My brother is." Well, that really sucked. "Yeah, you have no idea. He's coming in now. You don't have to worry about him either. He's one of the good guys. But be gentle with him, he's been hurt recently too."

She must have spoken out loud and realized that she was hurting more now that someone was willing to help her. When she looked at him again, his face had changed a little and she asked him about it.

"I'm the doctor. That was my brother Jorden before. I'm Kenton." Nodding made her ill, so she stopped doing that. "I'm going to give you something for pain. Are you allergic to anything?"

"Bullets." He didn't laugh, and she was pretty sure that it had been a joke on her part. "Just fix me enough that I can get rid of this voice in my head. He's making me crazy."

"Yeah, voices in your head will do that." He was humoring her. She had no idea why she though that, but found that she didn't care for it. Slapping out at his hands when he tried to pull her shirt up, he told her to behave.

"I need to get out of here." She didn't have any idea how that was going to happen, but she really did need out. "Just cut my finger off, take the ring, and I'll die a happy person."

"There will be no finger cutting off. Just lay still and let me give you this." He was too bossy for her, and she tried to slap him away again, but felt the soft glow of drugs as they entered her system. "Just relax and let it work."

"They'll find me." He asked her who. "I don't know. But this dragon told me that when they found me, they'd kill us both and anyone that…what is that you gave me? I feel fantastic."

"What dragon? Who told you about the dragons?" Emma wanted to tell him about the man in her head, but she was feeling too good to let go of her buzz. It was the first time in weeks that she didn't hurt. Letting the drug take her under, she saw the dragon for the first time.

There you are. He only nodded at her. *Where have you been? Do you know what sort of trouble I've been in?*

I do. But it is not over as yet. She asked him why. *I will not be able to explain it to you as well as I can show you. There are things put in motion now that neither of us can control, not now at any rate.*

The woman came into her view, older but still beautiful. She was standing in front of the doorway of a house talking to someone…two men. Emma couldn't see who they were, but she knew that they were vampires. Why she knew that when there was no such thing as vampires she had no idea; she only knew that was what they were. Then the woman fell back. The hole in her chest was bleeding badly, and Emma knew that she was dead. When she turned, Emma looking in the direction of the man's voice, she wasn't really surprised to see her brother Bart. But there was something wrong with his face. He was…burnt.

"You did this to me, Emma. It's all your fault that I look like this. Come to the hospital and let me kill you." She knew that it wasn't him, on some level, and that it was her mind. But the woman; Emma knew that she could help her. "Did you hear me, Emma? I said to come to the hospital and let me kill you. Then all will be right in my world. You know as well as I do that my way is the only way. It's the way that Daddy would have wanted it. Now, come see me."

He got up then and walked toward the woman. It occurred to Emma that she was seeing this as if she were in the room too, and knew that couldn't be it. She didn't know this person that was dead on the floor, and for some reason, Emma thought her brother didn't either. And where did the vampires go? When Bart kicked the woman, knocking her body over, Emma cried. For some reason, and she had no idea why, Emma thought she knew her. That somehow the woman was connected to the ring and the dragon.

You must help them. She asked the dragon how. *You will need to help them when they need it. Take them the ring and you'll know what to do with it.*

She's dead. I can't give her anything. He told her that if she ran again, that she would be. That helping them, the woman's family, would do so much for them all. *You mean I have to find them and give them the ring to save her? I can't even get the fucking thing off.*

Please help them. They need you more than you can know.

Emma wondered as she started to reach for the blanketing effect of the drug when anyone would care about her needs.

KATHI S. BARTON

Chapter 3

Kenton watched his mom. She was upset, yes, but thankfully this time it wasn't at him. He'd been in trouble with her for the last three days, since he'd been stabbed, and he was glad to let someone else take some of her anger. When she turned to him after pacing for five minutes, Kenton tried to think if he'd missed something.

"You don't know her." He said that he had no idea who she was. "And this dragon, you don't think she was talking about yours?"

"No. I don't know why, but I think she was out of her head with pain and infection. I had to clean the wound three times before I finally got it to respond to meds. She still has a fever that bothers me a great deal, but I don't know what brought her to me or what happened to put her in that position." He had an idea, but he didn't voice it to his mom. "She's got four broken ribs and a concussion. I had to use forty-seven stitches to put her back together, and that's not counting what I might need to fix her leg, if I don't have to take it off at the knee. Wherever she's come from, it's not been a very clean place. I'd say she's been on the run from someone."

"Who? I know you think you know, so who might it be?" He reached for the newspaper on the table and turned to the second section. The news of the explosion had run its front page status and was now on the back pages of the paper. "You think this is where she was hurt? Why?"

"The burns were consistent with what might have happened to her there. And then there is the added information that someone thinks a woman matching her description was seen leaving the scene of the crime. I have no idea why I think so, but I'm sure it's her." He looked at the paper again before continuing. "She said that someone has been shooting at her, and she told Jorden that he couldn't help her or he'd be shot at too. I'm assuming that she's tried to get help before this, and only broke into my offices to get help without anyone knowing."

"Jorden said he heard the alarm go off and went to see about it. He told me that she was talking to herself when he found her. You think...what about this dragon she was talking about? What did she say?"

Kenton had a feeling that she knew something. Not sure what it was, he answered her questions as best he could. When she sat down, he knew then that he'd been right, she was aware of something.

"What's going on, Mom? This isn't anything that should bother you. A hurt woman has been set to rights and when she's better, I'll put her on the next bus out of town and she'll be safe from whoever is hunting her. We've done it before." She said nothing. "Mom? What is it you're not telling me?"

"I'd like to see her."

He nodded and stood up. The woman was in the clinic that was on his mom's property. The clinic had been closed up for about a decade, but he still kept it supplied, in the event that someone needed him there. As they made their way to the building, he tried again to get her to tell him what was going on.

"I'll tell you when I see her. It might be nothing." He nodded. Kenton, like the rest of his brothers, would do anything for their mom. And he knew as surely as he was standing there with her that something was wrong and he needed to fix it for her. "This girl, did you say anything to anyone about her being here? That she spoke of a dragon?"

"No. No one but you and I and Jorden know about her. He helped me bring her here and then we spoke to you." She nodded. "Mom, you're scaring me right now."

As soon as she walked into the room, he knew that his mom was more upset than before. And when she took the woman's hand into hers, Kenton stood by helplessly while she sobbed. He asked her twice if she needed something and both times he only got waved off. The third time he asked her, his mom finally spoke.

"Remember a long time ago the story your grandda used to tell you about the demi-parvure that belonged to our family?" He remembered his grandfather talking about a lot of things, but not that. "Yes you do, only he called it a trousseau. Which was wrong, we found out later, and it wasn't wedding attire but jewelry, a demi-parvure."

"Yes, I remember. He said it was our heritage. A bunch of jewelry that once belonged to the queen of our kind. I think there was a ring, too, in the list." His mom nodded and showed him the one on the woman's finger. "You think that's the ring in it? The one that grandda talked about?

Mom, that was just a story he told us to have us dig around in the backyard. To get us out of the house."

"No, it wasn't a story but the truth. This is the ring." He asked her how she knew. "The stone would be as blue as the oceans from which we were born. The setting as golden as the sun that shown down on our wings. It would be as light as the wind that kept us high in the sky and as precious to us as the children we bore. I know this is it, Kenton. I know it."

He wasn't so sure. Kenton knew that there was this legend surrounding the jewelry. His grandda had told them there were six pieces of it. Necklace, earrings, bracelet, brooch or a pin, hair combs, and a ring. Kenton was sure there were no pictures of the things, but when he'd asked as a child, his grandda had claimed that he'd seen it and would know it like it was his own. But in all that time no one had ever offered up why they were gone, who had taken them, and what sort of reason there would be for them to have them back. He, like his brothers, had blown it off as a story from their beloved grandda.

"I can't get it off her." His mom asked him why he'd try. "Because it's more than likely not very clean. And if she has anything under it, like dirt or other bacteria, it won't help her to recover. I think if this ring were as precious as you think, she might not be wearing it like she is either. Right there on the first knuckle of her finger."

"I'm sure she has a good reason to have it on this way." He only nodded and watched his mom. "Kenton, what do you suppose brought her here to us? There had to be some force that had her breaking into your offices when she did. You said she spoke of a dragon and that it wasn't yours. Do you suppose she talks to something that holds the magic in the jewelry?"

"I'm a doctor and it stands to reason that I'd have something in the offices to help her. She broke in here because she knew that on some level she could get help on her own." His mom only looked at him. "Look, we can try and analyze this all you want, but we won't get any answers until she wakes up. In the meantime, I'm keeping her well and full of drugs so she won't hurt herself if she does wake. As for the ring?" He shrugged. "We'll have to wait on her answers for that as well."

When his mom left him, Kenton checked on the woman's leg and the rest of her wounds. He'd had to put in a drainage tube in her leg. The infection had been deep, and he wanted to make sure that he could clean it better. She would survive, he knew that, but what kind of story she had would be anyone's guess. He had a feeling that whoever was after her, if they found her here, then there would be hell to pay. But Kenton also knew that his family would not be caught in the middle of whatever was going on that would have her running like this. Ring or not, she wasn't going to bring anything down on his family.

Going to the smallish cot in the other room, he stretched out. He'd been staying there, close, in the event that she might wake. He didn't want her to wake and be frightened, and he also needed to make sure that she didn't run. And she would too, he'd bet.

The more he thought about how stupid she'd been to go for so long without proper care, the angrier he got at her. He really supposed it wasn't her fault that she'd been hurt, but he also wasn't sure that she was all that innocent of what had been going on there. Kenton wanted nothing to do with the family that had been in the building when it had gone up.

He knew the name Gentry as well as anyone did. Bart Gentry was a man to avoid. Even to be friends with, which his family had never been. But more importantly, they also knew to not be an enemy of the family.

When it came out in the paper that the elder Gentry had been killed, leaving his son badly burned, Kenton wondered what sort of things Bart had done to bring something like this to their lives. He knew as surely as he was a good doctor that Bart had had something to do with this. More than likely both the father and son, he'd bet.

Bart Gentry had gone to school with his brother Lewis, but they all knew him. Bart had been a bully and a bastard, thinking that whatever he wanted he should have, even if he had to take it from someone who actually owned it. So when he'd come upon Lewis, wanting the coat that he'd gotten for Christmas one year, Kenton and the others had stepped in and showed Bart the errors of his ways. It had been the most wonderful school detention he had ever received for fighting on school property. Not long after, Bart had been removed from the school and he'd never heard his name again until the newspaper said that his father had been killed in an explosion. And that the younger Bart was expected to make a full, but painful, recovery.

One of the doctors that Kenton had worked with said that Bart would be lucky if he was able to speak again, and that some of the burns would take years to repair, if they ever did. The burns to his body, he'd been told, were extensive. The man that had been found under Bart, Whitaker, had been burned as well, but he had been released from the hospital a few days ago. Apparently Bart had saved him from most of the damage. Kenton wondered what he'd think of that when he found out.

Kenton was thinking of the woman in the other room when his phone rang. He answered it, knowing that it was his brother Dalton. Dalton was a cop, a beat cop that loved his job more than he did most things. Kenton had asked him to do some searching on the mysterious woman from the building just on the off chance that he was wrong about her. He'd told him that he was just wondering why someone would run instead of getting medical help when she would need it.

"You are not going to believe this shit." Dalton was laughing as he spoke. "You remember that fuck that used to beat up the freshmen because he could? The guy who tried to hurt Lewis when he didn't give him his coat? Gentry was his name."

"I do, as a matter of fact. I was just thinking about him. Why do you ask?" Dalton was laughing pretty hard by then. "You want to share your good joke with me?"

"It's his sister. That woman that was coming out of the building that day? It's none other than his little sister. Didn't even know he had one, did you?" Kenton got up to look in on the woman in question. "Seems that they kept her under wraps in the event that Daddy ever had any trouble with the police. She was going to be his money bags. At least that's the way we're seeing it. Apparently everything that Daddy owned, and we're talking billions, belongs to her. There are any number of people looking for her right now. And not a great many of them in the best of humor about Dad dying off like he did. The only reason I found out is because there is this guy that is bragging all over the place that he was asked to test the DNA that was found at the scene. It matched the older Gentry's perfectly."

"You think she ran because she figured that they'd be after her next?" Dalton didn't know that she was hurt or that she was now in the house with him. "I would have thought that Bart would have been the next in line for his money."

"Yeah, apparently so will Bart when he finds out. He's royally pissed, apparently, that his doctors can't fix him up right now instead of waiting on him to heal a little. He has it in his head that all his money from his dad's estate should put him on the top of some list. I don't know what that might be, but he wants—demands—that he be as handsome as before. He's unable to speak, so he's writing everything in capital letters in that notebook that they gave him like he was in charge of the whole fucking staff there. They finally had to take it from him in order to take care of other patients. Oh, and Bart has been going through some pain meds too, the doc told me. More than they deem necessary for the extent of his injuries." Dalton called him a moron, and Kenton had to agree. "Anyway, I went by to see him yesterday, just to ask him about sister dear, and he's been burnt pretty badly. Lost an eye and an ear. Major damage done to his whole body, I was told. If infection doesn't kill him, he's in for some pretty extensive plastic surgery before this is all done. They're saying that he was pretty close to the blast site when it went off."

Closing the door to the recovery room, Kenton went to his desk and brought up the article about the fire and explosion again. For whatever reason this woman left the building, he was sure that it had a lot to do with her brother. Just what, he had no idea.

"Her name is Emma Gentry. Middle name is Anderson, like her mother. Her grandda is Baldwin Frank. You might have heard of him too." Kenton said that he had but was not sure where. "He's the guy who just bought up all the buildings around the outskirts of town. He and his family have been, in some form or another, linked to the mob as much as Gentry had been years ago, and then again recently. It's rumored too that they were forming a partnership when Frank's daughter was killed. Nothing much we've been able to find on that either. Why are you asking? I mean, just curious or is there something I should know?"

"She's here. Emma is here. But I can't tell anyone right now." Dalton told him that he'd figured that out already. "You knew she was here? How…? You know what, it doesn't matter. But I am worried for her safety. She's hurt too, but I have that under control as well."

"I'll come by later and see her. Not to talk to her…I don't want to know whatever she does. Not yet at any rate. But I won't say a word either. I think you might be right. She needs to be safe." Kenton told him of her injuries. "Call me if you need anything or see anything out of the norm. I'll come by tonight and look around too. Be safe."

After getting as much as he could from Dalton, they hung up. Kenton wondered what would make someone like her run. Would she have known about the money that was hers now and ran so she'd not have to share with her brother? Was she afraid of her brother, and that was why she ran? There were all sorts of unanswered questions running in his head, but he knew that he'd not get any answers until Emma woke up. To fill his time, he did some research on the Gentry family as well as the Frank family. Neither of them, mostly Bart on the Gentry side, were in good standing with anyone it seemed. And Kenton was just a little more afraid of having her there with his family.

~~~

Bart was in so much pain that he was sick with it. He couldn't see well enough to know who was in the room with him, but he knew that he'd better fucking get some answers soon. Like where the hell was Emma and why had she run?

"We've been looking since it came out that she survived. There is some talk about who she is, but no one has figured out yet that she is your sister." And Bart wanted to keep it that way. The less people knew about her the better it would be for him. Someone would take her and expect him to pay to get her back. Not that he would, but he didn't need the press right now. No way was he going to be standing in front of a camera looking like this. "I've got every doctor and nurse in the area keeping an eye out for her too. Even called in a few vets in the event she tries that angle."

Bart knew that his sister had not blown the building up around them. He'd done that. Only he'd set the timer wrong or something, so instead of it going off at ten at night when he knew his father and maybe Emma would be the only ones in the building, it had gone off at ten in the morning, catching him and the entire staff there off guard. Even his sister should have been killed, as he knew she worked until all hours of the night to just to keep up with the demands he put on her. Bart picked up the pencil that had been given to him when he woke up.

It took him forever to write a single word, and no matter how much he wrote it out, no one was giving him anything for the pain. He pressed the pencil to the paper again and wrote what he wanted to know. Mark, his only friend, leaned over the paper and read it aloud. Money? it said.

Mark had come out a winner in the building. Just a few burns and a broken arm. Bart was still trying to figure out how he'd been hurt so very little, but there was nothing forthcoming about that either. People were going to have to straighten up about shit when he got out of there. He was in charge now and they were going to know it. His daddy being dead left him in charge, and he was fucking excited about that.

"No. There is no getting to the money in the bank accounts that your father had. Not that I can figure out yet anyway. I can't find anything about wills either, or when someone might be reading it. It's like it's some big secret. He said that he didn't write it for your dad and so he had no way of telling me what was in it. I made sure he knew that if he did know, things were going to go badly for him and his family if I found out differently. Other than that, he said that someone would contact you if there was one. If not, then there would be a hearing and shit to determine who got what. I'm guessing he knew about Emma too. That's some fucked up stuff if you ask me." Bart wanted to scream, but could only close his eye against the injustice of it all. He was the oldest and the son; it was all his. "Hey, Bart, you think I can get some cash from your house? I'm running low, and you do owe me about ten grand right now."

Bart only stared at the man. He wished that someone would give him a gun, because right now he'd use it on this bastard. Asking for money from him at a time like this was about as callus as it got. Besides, Bart never paid people back…it was something that he prided himself on. If you were stupid enough to give him money, then you might as well kiss it goodbye. It was his now. But Mark was nodding like he'd answered him.

"Okay then, I'm going to take that as a yes." Bart picked up the pencil again, but Mark was backing out of his sight. "No worries about telling me where the key is. I got it. And thanks, man. I can't tell you enough how much I appreciate you paying up right now."

When he heard the door close, Bart threw the pencil across the room and wished that it had hit the man in the heart. This was really fucked up. Taking money from him was about as low as it got as far as Bart was concerned. Bart added Mark's name to the list of people that were going to be taught a lesson when he was in charge.

Bart had other things he had to deal with right now, and one of them was that he going to be deformed, they'd told him. Well, they'd not said it like that, but he'd lost an ear and his eye in the blast. Plus, there had been extensive damage done to his left arm as well as his left leg. Bart had been told that he'd walk again, but not without a cane. His arm would be just about useless too, as the fire had damaged all the muscle tissue there. Also, it was still up in the air whether he'd be able to speak. He wanted to look down at his broken body, but could barely move his head with all the things they had on his face. He'd been told that he was lucky to be alive. Bart wasn't sure that was right.

He'd been a handsome man, he knew this. Women had fallen all over him since he'd been old enough to fuck. Which he thought was younger than most men had. And he did whenever he got the chance. As he got older and pickier about his sex partners, he realized that he was really good at it. Fucking women had never been a sport in the Olympics, but he knew he'd be taking gold every time if it ever were. Maybe he'd rate in all three categories and make a sweep of it. He knew he was that good.

"It's time for your medication, Mr. Gentry." He wanted to tell her to double his meds, but his pencil was gone. "I wanted to let you know that the doctor will be in to see you in the morning, and if you have any questions for him, that would be the time to ask them. Oh, that's right, you can't speak yet." Her giggle had him jerking his arm from her. "You don't want the pain meds? Well, all right then." When she started to move away him without giving him the buzz he had come to crave, Bart grunted and begged for her to return. When she was standing in front of him, he memorized her face, because she was going to be the first person he killed when he was out of there. "Don't fuck with me, mister. I've got more important things to do than to care for a thug like you."

He was going to make her suffer. And he knew in that moment that she was keeping his drugs from him too. The doctor would have prescribed him much more than this bitch was giving him. Bart also knew that she was making a good bit of money off the shit she was keeping from him. Yes sir, he thought, he was going to make her suffer in ways she'd never seen before, and he was going to enjoy every minute of it.

As soon as the drugs started to kick in, he let his mind wander over the events that had brought him to this point. His father had cut him off a week ago. Told him that he was no longer going to support his gambling debts, nor was he going to be bailing him out anymore. And the drug money, the money that Bart had been collecting on his own, was going to stop as well. He was not that type of businessman.

"Why the fuck not?" His dad had only sat back in his chair and said nothing to his question. "You'll do this or I tell the world what sort of person you are. And you know that I know every little part of your life."

"And what sort of person am I, Bart? A mobster? I used to be, but I'm pretty sure that the world knows all about that. Or at least they think they do. And it matters little now anyway. I've been running a clean ship for years now, and all that is mostly behind me. It's you that is trying to make a name for himself on the most wanted list, aren't you?" He asked him what he meant. "I've been keeping an eye on you, Bart, and what you've been doing. As of this morning, all that is going to stop. Or at least where I'm concerned it is. And you'll not be hurting Emma any more. You lied to me about her too, saying that she had dropped off the face of the earth. When all this time you've had her hidden away, hiding her like an animal in the sublevels of this place. I more than likely am to blame a little on that, but I never dreamed you'd do that to myself and your own sister. Why did you do that? I'll tell you right now, had I known that was what you were doing I would have stepped in sooner."

"So what? Why do you care what's going on with her? She's nothing to us. Especially to me. Why do you even care what happens to her? She's about useless to you as a business man; not as good as I am anyway." His father told him that he'd been wrong about that too. "And now you think you're going to bring her into the family and what? Tell her how sorry you were for what's happened to her? Won't work. I've fixed that too. She thinks you hate her, and I'm sure she hates you too."

"I know." Bart was almost afraid that he did know what he'd been up to. "I've plans to explain everything to her. And once this entire thing with you is put to bed, then yes, I will ask her to forgive me. If she doesn't, then that will be on me. But you are no longer welcome here as my son. And I plan to look into your mother's death too. There has always been something that that seemed so wrong. I'm going to ask Baldwin to help me find her killer."

Bart had left the office about an hour later. No matter what he'd tried to get out of his father about what was wrong with the death of his mom, he wouldn't say. Nor would he tell him what he was planning to do with Emma. The fucking bitch had done this to him, he knew it.

He was still nervous about what he might have been thinking about his mom's death. Bart had been careful in that, making sure that nothing that had happened that night would ever come back on him. He wasn't even in the state when he'd had her murdered, and more than that, he'd made sure that the man who had killed her was dead as well. Leave no witnesses behind, his grandda had told him.

Now here he was hurt, and Emma was out there somewhere living it up like she had known all along that he'd be hurt when the building blew up. Well, when he found her—and he would—he was going to make it so that she was slave to him, doing what he wanted when he wanted for the rest of her days. And when he was finished with her, once she'd served her time, Bart was going to enjoy blowing her fucking brains out.

Then there was the ring. He had no idea why that kept circling around in his head since he'd realized that Emma had survived. He'd knocked shit off her desk all the time, and she had never bent to pick it up before while he was there. But this time she did, going after that fucking ring like it was worth something. He'd seen it, of course, shining right there when she'd bent over, and he'd nearly kicked her in the head while she was there too. But the rocking of the building had taken him, and he knew she had something that belonged to him. Like that fucking bastard Sebastian Logan.

He had taken something that he'd wanted. Not at the time, of course, but later when he'd heard from the one of the people that he did business with that a ring had been removed from the building without his okay. Emma had vouched for the man, saying that Bart had said he could have it. Like Bart gave a shit what she said. He was the boss of her, and the sooner she got that set in her head, the better off she might be. Bart had killed the man because he could, and had loved it every time his sister flinched when he brought out his gun. He loved scaring the fuck out of her. Until that last day, when she'd gotten uppity.

Bart was going to have to show her the error of her ways. Beginning with trying to take what was his again. First there was the ring, then her running off like she had something to hide or some shit. He wanted her here, making these people do what he wanted them to do. She was his slave, damn it, and now she was fucking out there on her own. She was going to die, and Bart was going to be the one to pull the trigger. No one fucked with what was his and got away with it.

Chapter 4

Emma heard the loud voices but didn't respond to them. Whatever they were talking about, it had little to nothing to do with her. At least she hoped not. Something about an injured boy and his grandmother. Emma hadn't really seen her grandfather but a couple of times, so hoped that she'd not fallen asleep somewhere and was having a bad dream. Why she'd dream about grandparents she had no idea, but she groaned when the voice in her head started speaking.

There is a young man by the name of Jim that has been hurt several times, and now his father is demanding that the good doctor tell him where he is. Why would she even care about that, she asked him. *Because it goes to show that he is a good man and one that you can get help from when the time comes. But he has hidden the young man and his grandmother away. Given them a fresh start is what he called it.*

I'm sure that he'll just be thrilled to no end to help me out. Opening her eyes, she realized that she was in some sort of hospital and looked at the two people standing near her. Both were men and related, but other than that, she had no idea. "Where am I?"

Just as one of them turned to her, she knew she'd seen him before. Where that would have been was a little fuzzy, but she knew him. When he smiled at her, showing perfect teeth, Emma could only think about the big bad wolf and how he'd gobble her up should he want too. Shaking her head caused her some pain, and he came to stand beside her to speak low.

"Kenton wants to you be quiet. He doesn't think it will be a good idea should Mr. Mason find out that we have you here. But I think if you went in there and kicked his ass, it would thrill a lot of people to no end." His breath was warm, almost hot on her cheek, and she moved away from him. "Do you remember me?"

"Yes. You're the man who found me in the clinic. When was that?" He told her. "I've been here for five days? Christ, they'll catch me for sure now."

He grinned at her, and she wanted to hit him for some reason. Emma knew people like him, thinking that if they were charming and sweet looking they could get whatever they wanted. Well, she'd turned down better looking men than him. Not many, but she had. She whispered to him that she needed to leave.

"Not just yet. My mom needs to speak to you first, and I'm not sure that Kenton is ready to release you either." She asked him why he had to release her. "He's your doctor. And he's spent a lot of time patching you back together, Emma."

Emma stared at the man when he said her name. She wondered how he'd figured it out and who he had told when he leaned to her ear again and told her that she was safe. No one was safe around her. She'd learned that the hard way over the last few weeks.

"Is my brother coming here?" The other man assured her that no one was coming for her here. "Yeah, and how do you know that for sure? I mean, I thought I was safe in the hotel, and someone came in shooting it all to hell to get me. Bart is not one to fuck with."

"Neither am I." The man that was standing in the doorway was also someone she'd met. The doctor. He'd told her that he was going to take care of her or some bullshit when he'd come to the clinic too. "Mason is out in the yard. You might want to call someone to come and get him. He's becoming a nuisance. Again."

The younger man left them. He was in a uniform, she noticed, and that frightened her more than anything. Kenton sat in the chair and the other man stood by the window looking out. She wanted to ask what was going on but was afraid to. Kenton cleared his throat and she looked at him.

"What do you remember about getting here?" Emma said nothing, but that didn't seem to matter to him. He knew everything, it seemed. "Seven days ago you were sighted in a hotel in Gilbertown. There you were hiding under the name Winder. Five people, including the cleaning lady, were shot and you escaped. They're not sure how you managed that, but you did. Only to turn up in a convenience store several hours later trying to shoplift some medical supplies. I'm assuming to help you with your wounds."

"I went to the hospital too. And while I was there, two people were killed. I'm not sure if it had to do with me or not, but I left." He told her that it must not have, because there was no word that she'd been there. "And how the hell do you know this?"

"Cameras. They're everywhere, and once word got out that you were being looked for, Dalton, the cop that just left, looked into some of the programs and we were able to track you all the way here. Well, not here, but to the convenience store that you were almost arrested in. After that, you sort of disappeared until you made it to my clinic." Emma leaned back on the bed and looked over at the other man. "I'm sure you remember him…it's my brother Jorden. He and I share the building you broke into that night. The other man, the one that left, is my brother too. His name is Dalton. He's on our side and is telling us when your name comes up on the wire. Which isn't as much as we thought, but then that could be because not everyone knows who you were when you left your father's building. We know because someone, a friend of Dalton's, put in a DNA order and it turned up you."

Cameras. She remembered what the voice in her head had said about knowing her but not. They were watching for her on cameras that were more than likely all over the place just hunting her down.

"So the three of you, you think to turn me in for some sort of reward? If Bart is putting one out there for me, you can bet that he has no intentions of paying you. Not with money at any rate. I would imagine that he'd expect you to die, not necessarily by your own hand either. He's not to be trusted at all." Jorden said that they knew him well enough to know that was true. "Good, then I have nothing to worry about. I'd like to go now. Please?"

"There are six of us, by the way." She asked Jorden six what. "Brothers. Kenton is the oldest, then me. Vance is third oldest, and then Dalton, Grady, and Lewis. Our mom is going to protect you too. She wants to meet you when you're up to it."

"Why?" Kenton asked her what she meant. "Why do you want to protect me? And more importantly, why do you even want to get involved with me? I mean, I broke into your business and you took me in. No one does that without a reason. What is yours?"

"We're all dragons." Emma could have gone her whole life without hearing those words. Not that she believed him, but she did wonder how he'd found out about the voice in her head and his claim at being a dragon too.

They are. And I am as well. These are the people that I have brought you to. Emma had no idea what to do and closed her eyes against the pain of it all. *They can help you.*

"There is this voice in my head. He claims he's a dragon. Or a part of one. He said that he's in the ring on my finger." Emma lifted up her hand and showed them the ring, and noticed that it was now on her finger all the way instead of just the tip. And there was something different about it. "He told me that I had to find someone for him and to return what belongs to them. This ring, he said, is part of something that belongs to you."

"Yes, a set of six pieces that belonged to my family long ago. They are what holds the dragon from us. What I mean to say is, because our inheritance was taken from us long ago, we cannot shift into our other halves. He remains a part of us, but not anything that we can pull. When the pieces are together, then he'll be whole and we can become what we always should have been." She asked him what that was. "Rich beyond anything we've ever dreamed."

It all came down to money. She supposed it was necessary to get along. She certainly could use a bit more now and then. Mostly now. Her rent was past due. There wasn't even a bag of Ramen noodles left in her bare cupboards, and she was pretty sure that her heat had been turned off. She glanced down at the ring again and thought about it and her brother.

"He didn't see it the way I do." Neither of them said anything, just looked at each other like they were having a nonverbal war over something. "All he saw was a band, worthless, and it pissed him off. Well, that's not really saying much. Everything pissed off Bart. But he told me that the man who he'd gotten it from said it was worth millions. But I could see it wasn't just a band."

"What do you see now?" Emma looked at the ring and wondered if it had really changed or did she just remember it wrong. "When you tell me, I have something I need to share with you."

"It was.... When I first saw it I remember thinking what a work of art it was. The dragon sat on the gold band with his body curled around the diamond. I knew it was a diamond when I saw it too. A whole carat, I think. But it looks different now. More...well, just more." Turning her hand, she studied the ring. "There are two dragons now. Their wings are the stems that hold the diamond. Their heads lay in a circle around the top, holding it securely. Not like before when I thought that it would fall out. The diamond is different as well. Bigger now and bluer. Before it was like a light blue, sort of along the lines of what people call baby blue. The blue of it now reminds me of summer days when you can't help but want to be out in the sunshine."

She felt fanciful, something that she never had been before. Emma supposed it was the pressure of her money problems and her family, but she felt stupid and wanted to lash out at the men who were keeping her here. But even as she looked up to tell them off, Kenton was looking at her like he was in awe over something. Money, she knew, could make people strange as hell.

"I want to tell you something. Something I'm not sure you're going to believe. The day before yesterday I was coming out of the bathroom there when I heard…I'd been taking a shower and I heard you saying something. I thought someone was here. You were having an argument with them. I came out of the bathroom less than fully dressed and you were thrashing around on the bed." Kenton stood up and began taking his shirt off. Emma knew that she should have told him to stop, but each inch he exposed made her want to see more. "You touched me. Well, you hit out at me. With your right hand. The one with the ring on it."

"I'm sorry." He nodded and pulled his shirt completely off. Her mouth dried up and her heart rate tripled. Christ, did all doctors look like this guy? And if so, why the hell didn't she go to see them more often? Jorden laughed and that set her temper off. "What the hell are you doing? Put your clothing back on."

Kenton moved toward her, and she squirmed. She knew that if he touched her, even to take her temperature right now, she'd be begging him to take her. When he reached for her right hand, it wasn't even an option for her to pull back. Emma watched mesmerized as he pulled it to within an inch of the tat on his chest. Just over his heart.

~~~

"I don't want to frighten you. And please, don't scream. My mom will come in here with guns blazing." Emma nodded at him, and Kenton had an almost overwhelming urge to kiss her. But he gently placed her hand over his heart and felt the heat consume him.

The dragon took him. It was easier this time, changing from his other self to the dragon. He also felt as if he had more control over him. Moving closer to her, Kenton was disappointed when she cowered back from him. He looked at his brother when he stood up out of the chair he'd sat in and moved toward Emma. Kenton, for the first time in his life, wanted to tear his brother apart. He stopped moving toward her when he growled low.

"I won't touch her." The dragon seemed to be okay with that, but no less cautious of the man. "Emma, in all our life, none of us have ever been able to shift before. Something about the magic not being there to make it work, like Kenton told you. Mom seems to think that the ring is what completed Kenton. The ring is the heart of the dragon."

The ring was…the man in her head, the voice had told her that he held magic. He'd told her many things, and most of it she thought was the ramblings of herself when she was alone. But he'd been right on things, a great many things that she would never have known. Like the fact that the building she was breaking into would help her.

"I don't want to be here. I'd like to go now if you don't mind. The ring is yours, of course, but I can't stay here." He moved closer to her and she moved back again. "Can you please ask him to not come any closer? I'm freaking the fuck out right now."

Tell her I'm sorry. Before Jorden could tell Emma what he said, the dragon started talking. It took him a minute to think he was saying things…the dragon was speaking to them both.

I am the heart of your dragon. The ring is the beating of my heart, and yours now as well. Your reward for bringing me here is this; the dragon within this man will forever change your life and you his. Emma said again that she wanted to leave. *Should you leave us, we will not be able to become what we are. The rest of me, all my other parts, need to be together to bring me out. You must stay with Kenton, this man, for me to be one.*

"I can't. I did what you asked. I brought you here. Now I'd like to go." The dragon asked her if she wanted her reward. "No. I don't want anything. I just want to change my name and move on so that I can have a life. Get a good paying job, maybe even go to the movies once. I want to have a life."

I will give you that and more. Emma looked at him, and he was surprised to see tears on her cheeks. Kenton hurt that she did, but he wasn't sure what he could do about it right now. *You brought my dragon to life. I don't know why, but I have a feeling that it had to be you that did it and none other. And when the other parts come, the rest of the set of jewelry, those pieces will bring the other dragons out too. All of us.*

Emma said nothing, but Kenton had a connection to her now. He could feel her emotions, her thoughts. He knew her worries and her fears too. Her life up until now had not been a good one. Even with being the daughter of a very wealthy man, she had nothing. Less than nothing really.

I can help you with your billings, get you a car that runs. I can even make sure that your brother never bothers you again. I want to –

"Can you be a person?" He had to smile. The tone of her voice sounded much like that of his mother when she was trying to make a point, and he was not getting it. "It's a little weird talking to you like this. Just be a person and I'll explain to you again why I have to get out of here."

Something that he'd learned the hard way yesterday was to keep his clothing on. He'd tried shifting in a small area, one where he could change into the clothing that had been brought to him. But the space was too small and he'd been nearly claustrophobic before someone managed to help him get out. That was just one of the many things he'd learned actually. Another one was that he could call out to his brothers. Not his mom for some reason. Also, and this one both disappointed and made him happy at the same time, he couldn't fly. He supposed that was something he'd either learn or it might not happen at all. Still, he let the dragon go and stood still while Emma stared at him.

"How do I get this ring off?" He told her that he had no idea. "It's not mine. And I don't want it. I was only supposed to bring it here to the owner, which I'm assuming is you, and I could go on with my life."

For some unexplainable reason that hurt. He tried to work through why it did when the dragon spoke. Kenton wasn't sure that his answer was going to be the one she wanted either.

You cannot remove the ring. Not ever. It is as much a part of you as young Kenton is now. He wanted to ask what that meant but Emma was telling him no. *You are what brought me here, to this point. And for me to be whole, all of me, you will all need to be here when the other parts of me arrive.*

"You didn't mention that when you said I was to bring you to this person. All you said was, I was to deliver the ring to someone and then I'd be rewarded. I don't care if you reward me, but I want you to hold up your end of the bargain." Kenton was hurting. His heart felt as if every word she said was a dagger to his heart. And when she continued, it was all he could do not to tell her to shut up and let him think. "I had a life. A shitty one, but I had one. I didn't want to be this courier any more than I'm sure that Doctor...I don't even know who he is, but I'm sure that he never bargained for some strange woman hanging around so he can be this other thing."

He is your reward and you his.

Emma tossed the covers off and started to rise. He'd meant to tell her the extent of her injuries and what he'd had to do to save her leg. The drainage tubes that had been put in were ready to be removed now, but he'd not had a chance as yet. She looked at him.

Kenton moved to her slowly...he didn't want her to jump off the bed and tear up the work he'd done on her leg. Also, he didn't want her to be hurt for any reason, so carefully, he made his way to her as if she were a terrified child.

"You had a serious infection and I had to drain off the pus or you'd die. I cleaned the wound several times, but it had gone much too long for me to be able to just leave it that way. Do you understand?" Nodding when she did, he moved slowly in her direction. If she stood now, Kenton wasn't sure he was close enough to catch her when she fell. Because there was no doubt that she would. Her leg wasn't strong enough just yet. "Had you had care right away, you would have been healed by now. But with the burns and the dirt that got embedded in your leg and in your weakened condition, I had to do something drastic."

"There are hoses in my leg." He nodded and lifted her injured leg up and laid it back on the pillow. "Will they have to stay there forever?"

"No. I can take them out today. I'd like to wait another day or two, but if you will rest and stay off your leg, I can do it now. But if the infection returns, I'll have to put them in again." He pulled the sheet over her body and watched her closely. "You're on antibiotics as well. Strong doses that did wonders for your fever and the other ailments you got from the blast. And your ribs, I can see that you're breathing better and are healing nicely as well. All except for your leg, you're almost as good as new."

"My father was there, I suppose. I mean, I didn't see him at all, but he was killed there, I guess. The dragon told me."

Kenton knew that her father was dead. It was all over the papers. Also her brother's hospital stay was reported on almost daily too.

"You were worried that someone would come for you. I don't know who that is, but no one seems to know you were there. I mean, they're narrowing it down, but few knew that Gentry had a daughter. Much less that she worked in the building with him." She nodded and laid her head back against the pillow. Jorden left them then, and Kenton sat on the side of her bed to talk to her, reason with her if that was what it took to keep her there. "Once they find out you were there and a survivor, you're going to be hunted more than you are now. People are going to want answers."

"So do I." Kenton nodded. He could still feel everything about her, and when she turned to him, he wondered if she could feel his as well. "Yes. I can feel everything about you. And read your mind. I don't care for it overly much. You have a lot of sick bastards in your practice in the event you didn't know that."

"I do. Some aren't so bad; others I could do without. But I'm not here to judge, only to help." She nodded and told him he was full of shit. "Yeah, my mom says something like that as well to me. McCade, by the way. My last name is McCade."

She didn't say anything, and he wondered if she was going to leave it. He then left her to go and get his mom. She had said that she'd come by when Emma woke up, and so instead of going for her, he reached out to her and told her that Emma was awake. She asked him if she was all right.

I believe so. Overwhelmed, but then so am I. Emma looked at him again. *I think she can hear us talking. I'm not sure.*

"I can." Emma turned away from him then, and he wanted to pull her into his arms. "Tell your mother if she wants to talk to me, that's fine. I'm not sure what I can tell her, but it's fine if she wants to come here."

"She wants to ask you about the ring and the dragon. My mom believed in him first, by the way. Well, her whole life I guess. My grandda, her father, told us about him and the riches that were ours our entire life." Emma nodded but didn't look at him again. "Her name is Aisha McCade. You can call her by her first name, but not Mrs. McCade. She doesn't care for that overly much for some reason. She's one of the sweetest, most fearsome people you'll meet."

"Because I didn't care for my mother-in-law. Her son much either, but I won't even go into how much didn't care for the man. Except to say that he gave me six wonderful boys to raise." Kenton stood up when his mom entered the room. "Hello son. Been spreading lies about me, have you? I am neither sweet nor fearsome. I can be stern when necessary, but I'm never sweet. Kenton, you may leave us now."

He wasn't sure that was a good idea. Emma was upset and he wasn't sure what her temper was like. Would she lash out at his mother? Would she try and hurt her? When he realized they were both staring at him, he felt his face heat up and he moved toward the door. But he went back and kissed his mom on the check, then did the same to Emma. He wasn't sure why he'd done it, but as he made his way out of the building and into the yard, he was glad that he had.

Dalton was talking to Grady when he entered the yard. It didn't look like something he needed to be involved in so he sat on the rocker on the wrap around porch with Lewis. He asked him what was going on.

"Grady is under the impression that he is something of a whiz when it comes to computers. Dalton is telling him that not only is what he's doing criminal, but it could get him some jail time. I think the discussion has gotten a little heated now that Dalton told him that he was going to arrest him the first time he hears anything about someone hacking into the police computer system again." Kenton asked if Dalton thought it was Grady. "Oh, it was him. He even admitted to it. Said that they have an antiquated system that is begging to be broken into. I think perhaps Dalton took offense to that. Or that could just be me."

Lewis, of all his brothers, was the most laid back, easy going person he knew. Little seemed to ruffle his feathers. He had rarely got into trouble when he was in school, and was usually the one that calmed things down between all of them when there was about to be bloodshed. Like he was pretty sure was going to happen between Dalton and Grady.

The scuffle broke out just as their mom came out of the clinic. She looked upset but only snapped her fingers and both Grady and Dalton stopped in mid-swing. Both of them looked as guilty as he'd ever seen them. Mom looked over at him and Lewis before she let out a long sigh and spoke.

"I need the six of you to get ready for dinner. We're having a family gathering and there will be no excuses as to why you can't make it. You will make a good impression on this woman and you will show up dressed like you know I want. Do I make myself clear?" The four of them nodded, and Kenton started to ask about Vance and Jorden. "I've spoken to Vance. He's coming in today and Jorden is on his way here now. If you make me pissy, you know there will be hell to pay."

After a chorus of "Yes, ma'am" they all moved to their respective vehicles. His mom looked at him, and he started to ask her what had happened when she shook her head. Whatever it was, he knew that she'd only let him know on her terms and not before. As he started for the clinic, his mom called him back.

"She has nothing." He knew that and told her. "No. I don't mean personal items, though she has none of those either, but she has no one to help her. A brother that she hates, a father that she doesn't understand or know and now never will, and more heartache than I've ever seen on a woman before. Kenton, she's going to need you to be…I was going to say understanding, but it's more than that. She is overwhelmed and doesn't understand why anyone would help her. Much less be there for her. She expects everyone to take advantage of her even when she has nothing they want."

"Mom, what is she to me, do you know?"

His mom patted him on the cheek, and he was reminded of times when he'd been little and she thought he should know the answer to his question and knew he'd figure it out. Eventually. When she walked away from him, Kenton found himself torn.

Did he go to his mom and ask more questions she wouldn't answer, or go to the clinic and try to figure out if Emma knew? He had a feeling that he'd get more information from his mom, but it would be hard. Emma might hurt him, of course, but she was easy to look at when she was angry. Smiling, Kenton went to the clinic. She might hurt him, but he'd have a lot more fun, he thought.

Chapter 5

Bart tried not to think about what the removal of the bandage meant. He knew that someone was changing it, the dressing they called it, but he'd been put under and he liked it that way. He knew that he'd be scarred. He also knew that he'd have to have cosmetic surgery as soon as possible. Sooner if he could get these bastards to do it. There was no way he was going to be able to conduct business looking like a freak. So when the doctor told him to close his eyes, he wanted to scream at him that he only had the one.

"I want you to know that you're going to look bad at first. The wounds are raw still and are going to take some time to heal. In about a year you can start having some other surgeries done to—" Bart started shaking his head, and the doctor told him to calm down. "You'll not be able to do anything until all the wounds are healed, Mr. Gentry. There is still a chance for infection, and your body won't be able to take any more damage done to it right now."

Bart was seething. He'd show the bastard what he could and could not do. He was going to be as perfect as he'd been before this shit had hit the fan. And the more he thought about it, the more pissed he got about how the timer had fucked up. He was going to sue that company as soon as he found his shit to see where he'd gotten it.

The bandage came off, and he watched the doctor. He didn't say anything to him, and for some reason that pissed him off more. Bart hated people, especially ones that knew more than he did. Not that he'd admit that aloud, but he knew there were some people that were a lot smarter than him. Reaching out for his arm to jerk him around to have him tell him what he saw, the doctor simply took a step away and stood there. That was when Bart looked at the nurses with them.

The one closest to him had her hand over her mouth. She looked horrified. Bart wanted to tell her to get out, but since this thing had happened, he'd been unable to do more than just grunt. He avoided doing that as much as possible, as he thought it made him sound like he was deranged. Then he looked over at the other one.

She looked sick. Her hand was over her mouth as well, but even Bart could see that she was close to losing her lunch. Before he could think how to get her out of the room and away from him, she leaned out of his vision and he could hear her retching. Bart looked at his doctor, who was still staring at him.

"The damage is extensive, as I have said." Bart wanted a mirror. Then he didn't. When the doctor suggested one, it was all Bart could do not to beg for them all to go away after covering him up again. "Now, before I show you, you have to understand that when you came in you were burned badly and some of the damage was irreparable. You know that you lost the eye and ear, but there was extensive damage done to the remaining tissue as well."

The mirror was suddenly in front of him. Bart immediately closed his eyes, not sure even now that he could look at himself. When he opened his eye and looked at the meat in the reflection, he knew that someone was playing a cruel and disgusting joke on him. There was no possible way that this thing looking back at him was him.

His eye socket was gone; it looked glued shut, like one of those masks the kids wore at Halloween, cheaply made and bunched together. His face looked like wet rubber or melting plastic. The doctor explained how later there could be an artificial eye put in if things healed the way that he thought they should.

His cheek was a mass of red puckered flesh. Blisters were still there, small ones, as well as some as big as a quarter. The brow had been singed away over the bad eye, and the hair on the side of his head was gone. In its place was nothing more than more stringy flesh that looked like someone had made it from wax and smeared it over him. His upper lip was missing. It was a part of the mess his cheek had become, and his nose looked to him like someone had smashed it to his face and didn't even bother putting in an air hole for him to breath. On top of that, if that wasn't bad enough, it looked as if the entire side of his head had shifted lower than the other side. Bart looked at his doctor.

"You're going to lose your teeth on this side as well. The jawbone was damaged enough that it's brittle and won't be able to support the teeth there. Your tongue, as you've been told, is also severely damaged so that you won't be able to talk without a slur. Drooling will also be an issue you'll find, but something that you can live with." Bart heard the door open and close, and realized that he could not smell the nurse's mess. Then he looked back at the doctor, who seemed to understand what he was thinking. "The receptors in your nostrils are burnt from the fire. Smoke inhalation has also damaged your lungs. You can get surgery, as I have said, but you will never be able to repair the damage that was done internally. I'm sorry."

Bart threw the mirror at him. He wanted to yell and scream—needed to, really—but all he could do was grunt, like an animal, like the monster that he'd become. This wasn't fair. This was not the way it was supposed to be. He should have been in bed, at home, when this broke out, and here he was suffering the most from it. Damn it, why didn't this happen the way he'd planned for it to? Why did he have to suffer when his father had been so lucky and had been killed? It wasn't fucking fair.

Bart needed for them to be gone; he wanted to think, to plan, and tried to make them see what he wanted. As the bandage was put back in place, this one cooler feeling than before, he tried to keep his mind from dwelling on what he'd just seen, how hideous he looked now, and what kind of pain he was going to have to go through to look good again. Because as surely as he was lying there, he knew that he'd be his old self again soon.

When he was alone, he wished that he'd asked for the mirror again. He didn't really want to see himself, but he was sure that in some way he'd missed something. Or the doctor had. There was no way that the face of the creature looking back at him was really his. Looking down at his arm, the one still fully bandaged, he wanted to sob for the injustice of it all. When the nurse came in and asked him if he wanted anything for pain, he could only nod at her. He wasn't even going to waste his time trying to put her in her place again.

He must have dozed off at some point. The room was no longer brightly lit with the sunlight, and there wasn't much in the way of sounds coming from the hallway. Bart really wanted to believe that it had all been a nightmare, but he knew, somewhere deep in his heart, that it was all true. He was a monster.

"Hello, Bart." The voice didn't sound familiar, and turning to look at the man there was nearly impossible with the way his flesh pulled at him. "Christ, but you should have died back then. You look like shit. Have you had the opportunity to see what you look like? You are truly the monster I always thought you were."

The light flared on, burning his eye, and he looked at the man in front of him. He knew who it was but couldn't for the life of him know why his grandda, especially after all these years, would come to see him. He'd not had a thing to do with the man since his mom died, for good reason too. When he stepped closer to his bed, Bart could see that he wasn't alone. There were two other men with him. One of them was Mark, his friend, and he looked like he'd been beaten to shit.

"He's been most helpful, your friend. Imagine my surprise when he came to me with all the answers that I had previously not been able to figure out. Well, come to me isn't really what happened. We were keeping an eye on your house and, lo and behold, he shows up to rob you. He just happened to mention, too, how you were the one that killed my little girl." Bart looked at Mark, then back at his grandda. "You know, I've been blaming your father for this all along, and here it is, resting on your doorstep."

Bart watched in horror as a gun was put to Mark's head and he was shot. The sound, a small puff, was all that he heard as Mark dropped to the floor. Bart started grunting and moaning as he reached for the nurse call button.

"Won't do you any good. They're all on my payroll as well, as of an hour ago." Bart looked at the monitors that had previously brought them running when he'd been in pain. "That won't work either. I've taken the liberty of fixing those for you as well. Steward here is very calm, don't you think? His heart rate never moved up a button when he killed that man. Amazing control, don't you think?"

Steward, the man with the gun, pulled his shirt open and showed him how all the tabs had been put on his body. Bart looked down at his own and saw splatters of his friend's blood all over him. He looked back at his grandda when he sat on the edge of the bed.

"I had hoped when I blew your place up that you'd be killed. But I think I like this idea so much better. The poor man loses all of his good looks, goes a little insane, and kills his buddy in a fit of rage over a woman. I especially like the part where you're going to kill yourself over the fact that you just don't think you're pretty enough." Bart shook his head. There was no way he was going to do this. "And don't think I can't make you do this, Bart. I'm a man who gets what he wants. And having you dead is what I so dearly want. But I would like to ask you where my ring is. I'm assuming that you spent all the money. Last fling, I guess you could call it now. But where is my ring? The one you stole off of my men?"

The man who had just killed Mark stood over him and put the gun to his head. Bart knew as surely as he was laying there that this was the end of his life. Before he could beg, even if he could, his grandfather laughed. Then the gun was suddenly gone.

Cruel joke. One that Bart decided that he was going to make the man pay for as soon as he could. To do this, to a man like him who had nothing left but his life like a monster, was beyond anything that Bart would ever do to a person. Or so he liked to think for the moment.

A pen was shoved in his hand. Then a sheet of paper was under it. He tried to think where the ring had been. Then he remembered. Emma had been picking it up when the building had blown up around him. Bart didn't give a shit about her enough not to simply throw her under any bus that kept him alive, so he wrote her name down.

"Your sister has it. Figures. Now, Whitaker tells me she had as much to do with killing my daughter as you did. That it was all your idea, but she went along with it. He said it was because Anderson told you no, that you could not kill your own father and then take over the family business. Is that true?" Bart had no idea what part he was supposed to answer, so he just nodded. "Good to know. You kept it all in the family, didn't you? She sounds as conniving as good old Dad and you, doesn't she?"

The gun was shoved in his hand and he lifted it and pointed at his grandfather. Pulling the trigger did nothing more than click at him, and both men laughed. Again with the cruelty, and he wanted to get up from the bed and kill both men. Before he could do much more than just lay the gun on his lap, another one was put at his head just as his grandfather stood up. He was at the door when he turned back and nodded. Bart watched in horror as he left him.

He felt the touch of the gun to his head again. Looking up at Steward, he thought the man said he was sorry about this, but he was on the wrong side, the side where he had no ear. Bart wanted to beg him not to do it, but he wasn't sure how.

Bart actually felt the pain of the bullet enter his head...then nothing.

~~~

Emma was just trying to figure out how to get out of the stupid bed and to the chair when the door was opened and there stood two of the men she'd met last night. Grady and Lewis were looking around the room as if they expected something to jump out and get them. Then Grady came to the bed and leaned over her.

"There has been an incident at the hospital and we have to move you to be sure you're safe." His voice was calm, but she could hear the underlying fear there. Whatever had happened, it wasn't going to be a good thing. "Your brother is dead."

"Who killed him?" He looked at her oddly, and she had to remember these men didn't know her brother these days. "He's not a nice person. I know you're aware of that, but over the last years, he's made some pretty powerful enemies. I'm one of them, but as you can tell, I'm not able to go there and do the killing myself."

Grady grinned. "Note to self, don't piss you off. And he is supposed to have done it himself." She started to ask him what that meant when he continued. "There are men in suits at my brother's office and they're asking him if he treated you. Now, normally that wouldn't be an issue for him in lying to them. But you see, these men aren't human either and know that he's lying."

"Not human. As in...more dragons?" She was still having a hard time wrapping her mind around the fact that she was currently staying with a dragon, but Grady just shook his head. "I see. And what are they? Werewolves? Ghosts?"

"Vampires." She glanced over at Lewis when he answered her question. Well, he'd not really, but he was grinning at her. Emma thought she liked and was afraid of Lewis the most of all the men. He had a quiet quality about him that made her think of henchmen in movies. "Some have the ability to tell when a person is lying or not. Kenton isn't sure if these guys have it or not, but he doesn't want to take any chances."

"I see. Actually, no I don't. But be that as it may, why are you both in here when I know you didn't come here to tell me about vampires and men in suits?" She looked at both of them when they didn't answer her. "Tell me, or so help me, when I'm better I'm going to hurt you both."

"Someone sent them to find you, and they're not the police. And, as your brother is no longer alive, we can only assume that they want to make sure that you're not either." She asked Grady why they'd care. "Because you're a Gentry."

"You know, that's the dumbest thing I've ever heard." Lewis nodded and stood by the door. "Okay, besides my brother being dead and mind-reading vampires at Doctor McCade's office, what does any of this have to do with me?"

"We don't know." Again, she wanted to hit one of them but waited as Lewis seemed to be thinking things over. "Okay. I guess we need to tell it all to you, but for now, we have to get you out of here."

"All right." She started to pull the sheet off when she was suddenly in Grady's arms. "If you could just lend me a car for a few hours I can leave it somewhere and you can claim you don't know what happened to it. I don't need any money, I guess. I've never had any before and got by."

Her mind was going a million miles a minute. They were shoving her out the door was all she could think about. Not that she blamed them. If men in suits were coming, then the entire family would be in danger. And as much as she didn't want to be hurt, she didn't want these people to be hurt or killed either. She was essentially alone in the world right now. But when he bypassed the car and moved up to the big house, she asked him what he was doing.

"For the moment, I'm taking you home, to our mom's home. And if you argue with me, Kenton said I was to remind you that he's a dragon and can eat you alive if you do." Grady laughed. "Not really, but those men are going to come here. He knows it now and he can't come to be with you."

"Why would he even want to? And why do you?" He looked at her oddly, but she was still trying to figure out what the fuck they were doing. When she was sitting on the couch, Mrs. McCade came in with a large box and smiled at her.

"They're expecting you to be banged up and out of shape." Emma nodded. "This is what Kenton suggested we do to hide you in plain sight. I think it's a wonderful idea and I cannot wait to see you dressed like this, but we have to hurry."

The box was opened and a huge body like thing was pulled out. When Mrs. McCade turned it toward her, Emma could see that it was a very pregnant belly thing attached to huge boobs. It took her mind a few seconds to catch up to the rest of them.

"You're going to make me look like I'm a hippo?" Mrs. McCade told her no, just large with child. "I see. And this will tell the men who can read my mind what? That I'm a Gentry that likes looking like she's about to pop?"

"Oh no, dear. Nothing like that. They can't read your mind, not when they get here." Emma asked her why not. "Because this house, like all the boys' houses, is special. We must hurry. I'll explain it while we work. By the way, you're Kenton's wife."

As the body thing was put on her, things started to fall into place. The men were coming here to kill her. Why? She had no idea, but she'd learned being related to Bart that it mattered little what the main reason was for killing so long as they got a thrill about it. She asked Mrs. McCade why there wasn't any way for them to read her mind. That one she just couldn't understand.

"Long ago, my husband captured a faerie. She wasn't really keen on my husband for that and many other reasons...he wasn't the nicest person in the world. But that's another story, and she did like me. Anyway, she saw the way that he treated me and the boys and put a ward around this house. No magic other than our own will work here. Verbal magic will work, but I'm not sure how as yet. My husband...he's dead now, but he wasn't able to control us with his own type of magic, and I believe that it saved us a lot of pain and suffering at his hands."

Emma looked at Mrs. McCade then. And that was when she noticed the long scar on her forehead. It was thin and someone had done a good job sewing it, but she'd bet anything that he'd done that to her. Emma put her hand on hers and looked her in the eye.

"You killed him." Mrs. McCade...Aisha...nodded after a moment and Emma nodded too. "I wanted to kill Bart so many times in my life. He was cruel too, and hit me when he could. Then as I got older, the suffering came in other ways. More sadistic, you might say. It's why I have nothing. He would pay people to come to my house, beat me, and take my things. Food, clothing, anything and everything, including furniture that wasn't too heavy. It's hard to get to that point, the point where it's you or them, and you know it."

"He'd only ever hit me at first. He'd scream and yell at the boys when they did the slightest thing wrong, but he'd never hit them. Then one night, he came after Lewis with an ax. He'd been...Lewis is so quiet and he thinks things through before he says anything, and his father hated that about him. Also the fact that he never seemed to get mad. But that night he did. He'd hit back at his father, and that had made him angrier than I'd ever seen him." Aisha looked at her son now. Lewis was her baby, and Emma knew that. "He was going to cut his head off. Had him down on the floor to do it, his booted foot at his chest. As he drew back, I shot him. Dead. I've never regretted it once that I did it, either."

"Good for you. If I had stood up to my brother, he might have done things differently with me." Aisha said he more than likely would have killed her. "Yeah, probably. But then, who cares?"

"I do." She looked over at Lewis when he spoke. "I care that you're here. That you and my brother are going to be together."

Before she could correct him on that, Grady came into the room and said that they were here. Coming up the drive now. Emma slipped on the suit and sat down, the huge shirt she'd put on smelling like Kenton.

Taking it to her nose, she drew deeply on the scent. There was something very delicious about the man's cologne. As she put the shirt to rights, she looked at Grady when he laughed. Asking him what was so funny only got more laughter from him, and she wanted to punch his nose. All the violence that she had felt before seemed to have dissipated with the death of her brother.

Two men came to the door and were not invited in. Emma stood near the table that was in the entrance hallway and leaned heavily onto it. Aisha spoke to them through the open door that seemed to be wider than was necessary for the two men. She wasn't surprised when one of the two asked several times to be invited in.

"No." Emma had enough of their being bossy and moved to the door, limping as little as she could. "What is it you want here? To come in? No, that's not going to happen. We don't want you here anymore than we'd want any of your kind."

The bigger man snapped his teeth at her, and Emma growled low in her throat. She had no idea why she did it, but he stepped back from her and the door. Putting her hand on her fake belly, she stood in the doorway, giving Aisha just a little nudge to get her to step back.

"We want to know if the woman by the name of Emma Anderson Gentry is here. If she is, which I do believe that she is, we want her to come out of the house so that we may speak to her." Emma cocked a brow at the man. "You will do as I say and answer me."

"Fuck you." Emma heard Lewis laugh and wondered about that, but the man in front of her was pissing her off. "Emma Gentry died the day of the explosion. Yeah, we know all about how she was there and how everyone thinks she got out. Tell me, have you been there? Have you had a look around? I'm pretty sure that nothing survived there but the cockroaches. Unless, of course, that's what you are. The cockroaches that crawl around on your belly terrorizing innocent people."

"Now see here, you can't talk to us that—"

She took a step toward him and felt something run over her skin. Before she could look at her arm to see what they'd done to her, they were both gone. Emma turned to the others in the room.

"You scared them." Emma shook her head at Lewis's statement. "Oh yeah you did. Scared the shit right out of them. And if I don't miss my bet, I'd say you showed them what you're made of as well."

"And what was that?" She'd meant the movement along her skin, but he took a slow step toward her and lifted her arm up. "Lewis?"

"You have his dragon."

Then the dream came to her. She looked over at Aisha and remembered her being shot in the chest, the way her body fell to the ground. The scar, the one on her forehead, seemed to shine now, showing Emma that this was indeed the woman that had been shot. The dragon spoke to her just as she was sitting her ass on the floor.

You saved her, just as I thought you would. The compulsion of the vampires, they could have brought her out of the house and then had her killed. The bullet to her head would have ended everything for them all. Emma asked him about her brother and reminded him that Bart had been there too in her dream. *He was here. His reckoning had been brought to you, and you now know that he will no longer bother you or this family again.*

If only it were that easy, her mind said just as she felt herself being swallowed up by the darkness. If only everything was that easy.

Chapter 6

Kenton listened to Lewis tell him what had happened twice before he asked him about the dragon. He could tell that Lewis thought it was funny for some reason, but all Kenton could think about was that they now shared something. His dragon.

It wasn't as if he didn't want her to have a part of his dragon, he told Lewis. He figured that she'd brought him out, so there was no reason to not share. But the fact was he was still trying his best to figure things out, and she seemed to have a handle on it all, whatever handle that might have been for her.

"You know that makes no sense whatsoever." He asked Lewis what he meant. "You just said that you didn't care if she had a part of you, but that you were jealous that she was better at it than you. Better at what? You think she knew what she was doing?"

"Yes." Lewis just shook his head. "You said that she went after those vamps like she meant it. How the hell did she know that they'd be afraid of her? Or for that matter, how on earth did she know to call the dragon out to scare them off?"

"I don't think she did. I think she was as surprised at that as the vampires were. But I would like to point out that she was there for us." Kenton asked him how. "They were dragging Mom through the door. And there wasn't shit either Grady or I could do about it. We were captured by their voice and all but Emma was hearing it."

Kenton wondered about that for a moment. "Mom seems to think that there is something there, something between Emma and me. I don't think Emma cares all that much for me."

"She does. I think, like you, she's not sure. Perhaps you should use some of that charm you use on Mrs. Bishop and talk to her." Kenton pointed out that Mrs. Bishop was ninety-four years old and loved his flirting ways. "Yeah, well, big brother, I'm betting that Emma will as well. If you don't, then I'm going to ask her out. I like her."

"Stay away from her." He had no idea how he'd managed to get across the room and have his brother in a head lock, but he didn't let him go right away. Instead, he told him that she was his. "If you so much as pretend to ask her out, I'll cut you in ways that your next girlfriend will laugh her ass off at you."

"Then fucking do something about it before she decides that waiting on you is a waste of her time." Lewis stood up when he let him go and turned to him as he continued. "She's beautiful, smart, extremely funny, and has had her heart broken more times than most. And all because of family members. She told Mom today that she has nothing. No home, no clothing, and no job. She feels that once she moves on, changes her name, things are going to start looking up. Especially now that her brother is dead. I myself can't imagine being excited that if one of you were gone, but she's almost giddy with it."

Long after Lewis left for his own home, Kenton sat on his mother's porch swing. He had never felt so lost around a woman in his life as he did Emma. She tied him up in knots tighter than he'd ever been since he'd realized that he could have fun with girls that didn't involve football or baseball.

He looked up when he heard the door open behind him. Emma was struggling to come out with a glass of tea and a plate of cookies in one hand, and her crutches, both of them, up under her other arm. He rushed to help her by scooping her up in his arms and putting her on the swing he'd been sitting on.

"You could have just taken the plate, you know. You guys are going to hurt something hefting me around all the time." He only stared at her, not sure if she was serious or not. "I only wanted to come out and enjoy the sun setting. I didn't know you were out here."

"You don't weigh that much. And being what we are, we're stronger anyway." He knew that didn't come out right and tried again. "We don't heft you. You don't weigh enough to be considered hefting anything."

"You are such a charmer." Kenton flushed and looked at the driveway when she leaned back on the seat. "Those guys that came here today, did Lewis tell you that they ran off for some reason?"

"He did. He told me that you have my dragon with you still." She nodded and ate one of the chocolate chip cookies before offering him one. Taking it, he decided to try the charm thing on her. "You're very lovely tonight. I think perhaps you're looking prettier all the time."

"Yeah? I don't think so." She looked at him. "I'm not much of anything. I mean, I know that I have all the girl parts and that makes men want me, but other than that, I'm not too much of anything."

"Girl parts?" Kenton laughed, he just couldn't help it. "I think you have very lovely girl parts. In fact, I really like all the parts that make you who you are."

"Are you hitting on me?" He told her he was trying. And he was pretty sure he was failing. "No. Not failing. But then I've never really been one that men hit on. Even before they found out what my last name was."

They rocked for a bit longer and he took another cookie when she offered. There were crumbs on her lip, just enough that he wanted to see if her mouth tasted like them. Would she be as sweet, as delicious as the cookies were? Putting the last of his cookie in his mouth, he chewed it slowly, trying to think what best way to kiss her. Then he thought, what the hell, just ask.

"Emma, I'd really like to kiss you. I mean, I'd very much like to do more, but kissing is a good start." She stared at him like she didn't believe him. Or she thought he was nuts. "I have thought of tasting you for days now. Mostly every hour. Really, every minute."

Yeah, that didn't make him sound any less crazed, he thought. When she looked away, Kenton wanted to tell her to forget it. That he'd only been kidding. But then she spoke, her voice soft and sad.

"I don't have a lot of experience with men like you." He asked her what sort of man she thought he was. "Good looking. Nice. Gentle when you have to be. I don't know a lot of men that still take the trash out for their mom, clean up their room, and even make their own bed. I usually, when I date, which isn't often, go out with the type of people...well, like my brother. Mean and mouthy. Hurtful and bastards. It's mostly why I never date. It's safer for me. And my bank account. Men like my brother expect me to pay for everything when they take me out. Like it's some sort of treat for me."

"You should be treated with respect and dignity. And so you know, I'm not like those other men, I'm just me. And as for taking out the trash and making my bed, I do that because, to be honest with you, I'm terrified of my mom." They both laughed, and Kenton put his arm behind her head and touched her, something that he'd been wanting to do for days now too. "May I kiss you?"

He watched her set the plate on the table in front of them. When she looked at him, all he could think about was not fucking this up. Kenton knew that this was going to be their first of many, or at least he hoped so. And first impressions, he knew, were the lasting kind. Pulling her gently to him, he touched his mouth to hers.

The kiss immediately became more. He'd not meant for it to, but hunger, for her, seemed to explode under the first taste of her mouth. When she gave him permission to enter, Kenton tasted more than just her sweet chocolatey breath, but all of her when he slid his tongue against hers. He pulled her closer when she put her hands on his shoulder. Pulling her closer still, he lifted her up and put her on his lap as he deepened the already heady taste of her and touched his hand to her breast.

His cock hardened to the point of pain. He tried to adjust her body so that she'd not notice that he was so hard, but she moaned when her fingers brushed over his cock. Kenton tore his mouth from hers and turned her around so that now she straddled his lap rather than just sitting across him. He was mindful of her wounds, but that was about all.

"I need to taste you." Nodding, she helped him pull at the buttons of the shirt she had on. As soon as she was bare to him, not even the lace of a bra in his way, Kenton lowered his head to her nipple and nibbled on the hard tip enough to have her curl her fingers in his hair and hold him there. It wasn't enough, he realized. He wanted all of her.

"Kenton?" He heard the voice, and he tried to get his lust-filled mind to wrap around who it was. When Emma nearly leapt off his lap and moved to the other side of the swing they were on, he grabbed the pillow from the side and put it over his lap just as his mom came out on the porch with him. "Kenton, I've been calling you. There is a woman on the phone that says she's in labor."

He started to rise and then stopped. Labor? He didn't have anyone even close to the beginning stages of labor. Kenton also knew that the service was on and that no one had this number. Looking at Emma, he could see her worry too.

"Mom, did she say who she was?" She said that she'd only said that she was his patient. "She's not. I don't know how she got this number, but it's not one of my patients. And if she is, then there is trouble. Call Dalton for me, will you, while I talk to her?"

"She's trying to get you alone." He nodded at Emma, not the least bit surprised that she got it too. "I think you should go. I mean, we should go."

"No, I don't want you hurt." She grinned at him, and Kenton thought of sharks and other scary things that could kill without provocation. "You have a plan then?"

"I do. This person on the phone, she might be a pawn in all this, but the men who have her think you're stupid. Stupid enough to just drop everything and come running to find out what she wants. It could be someone that you have as a patient, like I said, someone that might be held as hostage to have you come to them." He'd not thought of that and told her that. "Yeah, living with a bunch of criminals can make you suspicious about everything."

"So what should we do?" She grinned bigger, and he found himself thinking of her face when he took her to bed. Shaking that thought loose for the moment, he knew that he'd have to finish this before he could do anything even close to what he had in mind. "And by we, you mean all of us, right?"

"Oh yeah, all the boys, as your mom calls them. But she comes too. We don't leave a man behind." He nodded and winked at his mom. No, he'd not want her hurt either. Then Emma told him of her plans.

Yes, Kenton thought, this woman was going to be his before long. If he could convince her that he didn't just want her for her girl parts. Laughing, he listened to the plan and decided not to ever piss her off. She had an evil streak a mile wide in her.

~~~

Vance wanted to listen to the plan again. Not that he didn't get what they were doing, but he loved the way Emma got them all organized and ready for battle. He was sure it was going to go down just the way she'd explained too. The bad guy wasn't going to know what hit him.

"You ready?" He told Grady he was. "Good, because as much as I think this is going to work, I don't want anyone to be caught off guard with it. Where do you suppose she got such a great plan? Oh, and I'm never playing cards or chess with her. She's too slick."

"I won't either, now that you mention it."

He and Grady were in the room right off the examining room that Kenton had asked the woman to come to first before he had to go to the hospital. He and Grady were in town, and it was nothing for them to go in ahead of the family and wait them out. He heard the car in the drive and motioned for Grady to move to the door.

The plan was to see if the woman was in on it. Her name was on Kenton's roster of patients, and she was pregnant but not due for another three months. When she came by the door with a man, Vance saw the gun pointed at her back and relayed the information to Kenton.

I see her. As soon as I can get her.... He waited for Kenton to continue but when he did, it wasn't a plan to get the woman free but something he'd not expected. *There are three men in the lobby now. I'm not sure how they got in, but Emma just told me. They're reading months old magazines like it's giving them all of life's little clues, she said.*

Emma, looking very pregnant herself, was sitting in the lobby too. She had a phone and a gun. Vance wasn't so sure she should have the last thing, but she assured them all that she could shoot an eye out of a snake. He was sure she was making that up, but Kenton said she'd be fine.

Vance moved into the lobby as he'd been instructed if there were more players, and sat down on the sofa across from Emma, his back to the three men. When Emma stood up and stretched, he watched her as she pulled the gun out and put it on the back of the head of the man right behind him. Dalton entered the melee just as one of the other men was reaching into his jacket.

"Move and I kill you. Not a threat, in the event that you're wondering." Emma asked Vance to take their weapons, and he moved to do so. He was surprised to find not only were they armed with a gun each, but two of them had switch blades as well as a long thin piece of wire. He tossed those across the room with the weapons. She winked at Vance as she continued. "Check their boots. I saw that on a movie once, and always wondered if the bad guys really carried guns there."

Vance wanted to ask her if all of this was from a movie she might have watched, but was afraid of the answer. Instead, he reached into each man's boot and came up with three more guns, another knife, as well as a pair of brass knuckles. When one of the men's phones rang in his pocket, the man spoke for the first time.

"I think you need to answer that." He was looking at Emma when he spoke. "It's for you. Please answer it. It will go a long way to you understanding why we're here."

Her hand was trembling when she reached into his pocket. Vance wanted to tell her no, not to do it, but the man even leaned back and didn't say a word as she pulled it out. When the ringing stopped, so did his heart pounding, but only for a second. But the man smiled and said it would ring again. When it did, Emma answered it.

As soon as she sat down, he knew something had happened. Then the door opened from the outside and a woman stood there, a phone to her ear as well. Emma didn't move when the other woman put her phone away and didn't move either.

"These men work for me. If you'll let them go, we can help you with the two in the office with Doctor McCade." He and Dalton both looked at Emma, and when she nodded her head, the woman spoke again. "I assure you, they won't harm any of you. We will, however, take care of the men that are holding that young woman hostage."

"Let them go." Vance didn't want to do what Emma said, but when Dalton did, he backed away as well. As the men moved by them and to their weapons, he wondered if they had just made the biggest mistake of their lives. When the men moved again, this time to the hall and to the office that Kenton was in, he started to follow. "Don't. I have a feeling that we don't want to know what goes on down there."

"It's been a while, Emma. I was hoping we'd be able to sit down and talk." Emma said nothing, and Vance wanted to ask what the fuck was going on. "I'm her mother. She's having a hard time realizing that I'm not as dead as everyone believes."

"No. I'm having a hard time thinking why now? And why did you leave us? Not to mention, how did you know to come here, just when this was about to go down?" The woman sat down, and Vance stood by Emma. He could sense the tension between them. And when Kenton and a pregnant woman came into the room with them, Vance wasn't surprised to see Emma go to Kenton and hold him.

"What's going to happen with those men?" The woman, Mrs. Gentry, didn't answer. Vance had a feeling that Dalton didn't really want to know, but because of what he did for a living, he needed to know. "Am I going to have to explain this to someone higher than me?"

"No. No one will ever question you about what happens to them. The men, my men, will take care of everything." Mrs. Gentry looked around the room. "My name is Anderson Gentry. I'm Emma's mom and have been presumed dead for about seven years now."

"Did Dad know about you?" Anderson nodded. "I see. And were the two of you ever going to let me and Bart know? Or was this, too, one of your sick, twisted plans? You were good at them, if I remember correctly."

"No. I mean yes, but not Bart. Not until we had proof of his part in what happened to me." Anderson stood up. "If we could move to somewhere less conspicuous, I think I can explain this. My men need to move things around, and it would be better for all of you if you didn't know anything."

"You mean when they move bodies out?" Anderson didn't answer Vance, and he looked at Kenton. "You okay with this? This murdering spree that this woman's men are doing in your office?"

"They brought in a woman who is seven months pregnant, telling her that if she didn't cooperate they were going to cut her child out and then make her watch while they cut it up and fed it to the dogs. They threatened my life and that of Emma, as well as my entire family if I didn't do as they said, which was turn Emma over to them and keep my mouth shut." Kenton stood up, still holding onto Emma, and nodded at him before continuing. "Yes. I have no problem whatsoever in letting them do whatever it takes to make sure that no one is hurt by them again."

Vance looked at the sobbing pregnant woman, who had a bruised cheek as well as a large round belly. He said nothing to them as he moved to her, holding her upright as he told the rest of them he was taking her back to her home. After listening to Kenton, Vance decided he didn't have a problem with it either. But that didn't make it right. As he moved out to his car, he thought of all the things that were going on and wondered if love—if that was what it was— between Kenton and Emma was really worth all this.

As he drove her home, he noticed that Cindy, the woman, had a thick envelope in her lap. When she noticed him glancing at it, she smiled at him and told him that one of Anderson's men had given it to her.

"It's money. Enough that I don't have to worry about my child having diapers when he comes. Food on the table for my daughter. Nor will I have to fret about how I'm going to pay my rent when I'm off work. They told me that I should take this and start a new life, one that didn't involve being here anymore." She opened it up and he could see a huge pile of money. "They said it's $50,000. I only have to not tell anyone what happened. I can do that. I was afraid and hurt, but I'm safe now, thanks to you and your family, and I'll never tell a soul what you did for me and my children."

"She did it all. Mrs. Gentry." Cindy nodded and said she didn't care who it was, she was going to be safe. "I'm happy for you. But those men, they're dead now."

"Yes. And I for one won't lose a bit of sleep over it. They came into my home, hit me and my daughter. Then they made me make a phone call that had me lying to the most honest man I've ever met in order to use me to get him dead." She rubbed her hand over her belly and smiled at him as she continued. "Kenton helped me get medical care that I could afford. He helped me get out of an abusive relationship with my ex-husband, and he helped my daughter get into a daycare that didn't cost me more than I was making. She's safe too. No longer worrying about if her father is coming there to take her from me again. He helped me when no one else would. I'd do just about anything for him. And I know that he would me as well."

After Vance dropped the woman off, he could see what she meant about being safe. The neighborhood she was in was middle class. There were fenced-in backyards and swings in every one of them. He knew that looks could be deceiving, but he also knew that wherever she'd come from, Kenton had made this happen for her because he knew it was the right thing to do. Vance had admired his brother before this. Now he thought of him as his own special sort of hero.

Going back to his mom's house, he wasn't surprised to see that they all had gathered there. His mom would want that, being a part of whatever was going on. As soon as he entered the house by way of the kitchen, he was handed a drink and a plate and told to head to the living room. When he entered, he sat down and thought about the dead men again and realized that Kenton was right, that was the only way to handle this. He listened to Emma tell them what had happened seven years ago.

"Mom had been out with some friends. It was a weekly thing, something that she did to have her own time. Dad did his thing on Wednesday. Then on Saturday, they'd date. That Tuesday, there was a phone call from the police. An accident, they said. They told my dad that my mother was dead, died at the scene."

Emma started pacing, and Vance watched Kenton. He knew then that his brother was in love with the woman and smiled. Better Kenton than him was all he could think about.

"I'd been on the phone with your father. He and I were making plans for our weekend out when I was broadsided. I had only just hung up my phone when it happened, and I tried to reach for it to call your dad back. But two men got out of their car and came toward me. I don't think they expected me to have a gun." Anderson stood up and lifted her shirt to just below her breast. "I was shot twice. My leg had been broken in the accident, and I had hit my head. I killed the men, then called…. I had meant to call my husband, but I dialed my father instead. I was out of my head in pain and I believe he thought I was telling him that Bartholomew had killed me. It took me some time to recover, but I laid low until about three years ago. Bartholomew thought it best that we kept things quiet for a while. I think he thought that Bart set me up. Then we started looking for you."

"Me?" Emma looked around the room when her mother nodded. "I've been buried in that fucking building for years. Bart was my only contact. He told me that Dad wanted me there, out of his sight. I suffered all kinds of abuse at his hands, and why? So you could be safe and sound in Dad's arms?"

"No, we had no idea where you were. I never...we searched too. I thought for sure, and so did your dad, that Bart had killed you. As he tried to do me." Emma denied ever being anywhere but in the same building that her dad was in. "Bart said you'd run off. That you'd.... I guess we shouldn't have believed him about that either."

"I guess not." Emma stood up and then nodded to Kenton when he stood. "I'm not sure what is going on here. And right now I don't care. I'm sorry about...I have no idea why I'm sorry, but I am. I just need to think. When I'm ready, I'll contact you. Or someone will."

Vance looked at Anderson and could see that she was upset. He supposed she had a right to be, but he knew that he might be too if he was in Emma's shoes. This was just too bizarre. He decided that he was going to refrain from judging just yet. If she fucked with his family, which as far as he was concerned included Emma, she was going to be hurt. But for reasons that he could not fathom, Vance thought that Emma would die before hurting any of them. Anderson, however, he wasn't so sure about.

Chapter 7

Kenton followed Emma out of the room and to the front door. When she turned to him, if she was going to say anything at all, he didn't give her a chance to say it. Kenton pulled her into his arms and kissed her, giving her all his pent-up need and rage rolled into one. When she lifted her leg up, wrapping it around his own, he lifted her by her ass and took her to the wall. His need, like hers, felt too out of control for niceties. When she jerked his head from her mouth, he growled low.

"Do you have a room here?" He nodded and started to kiss her again. "Take me there. I don't want to have to worry about being caught again. Now, Kenton. I want you to fuck me on a bed where there are no witnesses."

The stairs were giving him problems that he'd never had before. As he held her and tried to navigate them, he kept getting distracted and missed steps nearly taking them both to the floor. Every time she touched him, kissed his bare skin, he had to stop. He knew it was either that or take her right there on the stairs. As they made their slow progress to the top of the longest staircase he thought he'd ever been on, he tore at her clothing too.

Her breasts, like before, were bared to him. He took one of the morsels into his mouth and suckled at her while turning the knob to his old bedroom. As soon as he was inside, he turned her to the now closed door and pulled the rest of her clothing off and set her on her feet.

"I want to do this right." When she reached for him, he backed up. "If you touch me now, I'm done. I mean, I'm so close to coming now that I can hardly breathe around it."

"I want you to take me." He nodded, then shook his head. "You don't want me? I thought...I guess I don't understand then why we're here."

"Christ, I want you. I've never wanted…. I don't want to just fuck you against the wall. I want to make love to you. In a bed. Properly." She grinned at him and he felt his cock burn with need to simply be free. "You're going to hurt me, aren't you?"

"I hope so." She moved to the bed, her body swaying in a way that had him stroking his full cock. "I'm going to lean over that bed right now and hope that you're going to join me. If not, I think I can take care of —"

He jerked her to him and flipped her onto the bed. As her giggles echoed in the room, Kenton pulled her to the edge of the bed and buried his mouth over her hot pussy. Her scream of pleasure had him smiling as he devoured her. Okay, so much for being a soft lover, he thought.

Her thighs tightened around his head, and he had to work hard at sliding his fingers into her. The harder he fucked her this way, the more cream that was his to have. When she begged him to stop, pulling his head up, he looked up at her and knew that at some point, he'd fallen in love with her.

"I love you." She nodded as he stood up. "I didn't know until this moment that it was possible to love someone as much as I do you."

"I fell in love with you too. I'm not sure when, but it seems like forever to me." He nodded and stripped off his pants. She sat up and kissed the tip of his leaky cock. "I want to taste you as you did me. Would you like that, Kenton? For me to take you into my mouth and let you come down my throat?"

"Oh God, yes. But you do and this will end now." Her giggle again had him smiling. "I want to fill you. Make love to you. Show you how much I love you."

"Take me, Kenton. Please?" He watched her move to the center of the bed. He wanted to leap on her, take her now, but making love to her was as important to him as his heart beating. Sliding into the bed beside her, he touched her, ran his fingers up and over her breasts while he watched her face. He touched her ribs, counting them as he went. Cupped her ass, loving the way that it filled his hand. Her thighs were a wonder, hard and soft at the same time. Calves that were muscled and strong twitched in his hands. When he kissed her navel, running his tongue into the deep crevice, she moaned with him. Kenton looked up at her as he moved around her on the bed.

"You're so lovely." He kissed the tip of her nipple. "And soft. I love the way your breasts tighten when you're aroused. And the color or your skin when you're excited. I can hear your heart beating too. Like you've run a long way and you need to rest a bit."

"You're killing me." He laughed and moved between her legs. He slid over her, his cock at her entrance, and he felt the heat of her pull at him. Kenton wanted to fill her now, take her hard and fast, but he really did want this to last. Kissing her as gently as he could, he gave her as much of his love for her as he could before slowly filling her. "Oh Kenton, yes."

Her body was accepting of his. She fit him, her sheath rippling along his cock until he had to pause before coming just as he was. Moving in and out of her, Kenton made love to her mouth, her throat, and ears. He loved the taste of her skin too, the heat of it, the dewy sweat as he took her. And when she cried out, telling him not just with her body but her voice too that she was coming, Kenton let himself go. Emptied all that he was inside of her.

Kenton held her to him when he felt his cock fill again. His heart was pounding so hard that he was sure she could hear it. So when she rolled him over, her body riding over his, he held her hips in an effort to keep himself from taking over again.

"I need this." He nodded as her body began to sway over his. Her hands cupped her breasts, her body hard with her need. "Kenton, I love you."

"I love you too." Her hips were moving faster, her ride out of control, it seemed. Rolling her to her back again, he fucked her, plowed her as hard as he could as he took her mouth in an almost brutal kiss. When he felt close to coming, Kenton had the most incredible urge to bite her, and he did.

The climax didn't just take him but overwhelmed him. He felt it from the tip of his toes to every hair follicle on his head. Even as he came, his body hard and stiff above hers, he felt his balls fill again and empty just as hard, just as completely. Her own peak pulled him under again until he felt as if he'd been drained, not just of his cum but of all of him. Kenton dropped on top of her, rolling to his back when he realized how heavy he was.

Neither of them moved. To be honest, he wasn't sure he could any more. As he held her in his arms, her body splayed all over his, all he could think about was that he had just had the most moving experience of his life. And that he couldn't wait to do it again. Smiling, he lifted her chin up to tell her again how much he loved her and realized she was asleep. Kenton thought that was a wonderful idea and closed his eyes.

~~~

"What do you mean, they're still alive? I thought you sent someone there to take care of them. What happened?" Steward handed him a sheet of paper and Baldwin didn't bother picking it up. "I asked a question I want answered, not a sheet of paper laying it all out."

"It's an email I got from Kenton McCade. It was his offices that we were going to go and take care of the lot of them in." Baldwin nodded, waiting for the excuses that he didn't want to hear. "He's not happy with the way things turned out. I don't believe you will be either once you read this."

"He killed them?" Steward told him no, not that he was aware of. "Then what the fuck are you talking about? Someone needs to explain to me why my worst enemy, a woman who killed my only daughter, is still running around like nothing happened."

"Our men moved in, just as they were told. The woman we used went with them, playing her part as well. Not willingly, but we had that under control too. Then we have nothing. No word from them. The woman and her daughter are gone, and there is no trace whatsoever of what might have happened at their house. I've had people watching the office building since yesterday, and that's all I know." Baldwin wanted to get up and kill the man, but knew that he'd have no more answers if he did. "Then today, about seven this morning, I get this email from him."

Steward picked it up and started reading it, to himself apparently. It was all Baldwin could do not to pull his gun out and end this shit. Then he started to read it to him.

"'Salutations, Baldwin. I feel that I can call you that, because presumably we're going to be related soon. You see, your granddaughter and I are seeing each other. You might remember her, she's the one you just recently tried to kill. Again.'" Baldwin wanted to give the man kudos for having balls, but he also was going to kill him. "'Emma and I want to thank you for yesterday. I don't believe that my office has been so thoroughly cleaned before. I never knew that blood could spread to so many places. It's a good thing there is a service that will not ask questions when you call them for that type of work. But I digress.

"'This is not really a warning or a threat. This is a promise. You come near my family again and I will make you regret ever being born. My family is everything to me. And rest assured, I will make sure that you understand that I'm a man that protects what is his.'"

Baldwin stopped Steward. "This man, what do we know about him? I mean, other than he's going to be dead soon."

"A doctor of good standing. Not a single skeleton in his closet that I can find. Pays his bills on time, doesn't have much in the way of credit, but he has a nice fat bank account." Steward took something from his briefcase. "Kenton has five brothers. All of them equally well thought of and having good jobs. Mother, Aisha, raised them pretty much on her own, as the father wasn't in the picture much. Abusive bastard, but he's dead now. 'Accidental' shooting is all I've been able to unearth on that."

"And he's hooked up with Emma now. Why?" Steward said that he didn't know what the connection was other than what he'd read in the letter. "So he's found himself in love with her. A daughter of a murderer, and that doesn't bother him."

"Apparently not. I would say that she's either hoodwinked him or she has found herself in a good situation. I doubt she loves him. If she's anything like her mother, I'd say she's just using the bastard to hide from you." Baldwin asked him why he thought that. "Isn't that the reason that Anderson married Bartholomew in the first place? To piss you off?"

"Yes. And see what that got her." He thought about his little girl and wondered what she'd think of all this. "Anderson claimed to have loved Gentry. And like a fool, I thought I could get him to do what I wanted because of that. But all he thought of was himself and what things would bring to him. Then all of the sudden, he just up and turns into a nice guy with morals. Fucking moron. I thought that was what got Anderson killed, but I wonder now if he was cutting ties with Bart when he found out the idiot worked with me and that was why Bart did it."

That was the truth. Baldwin really did come to believe that Gentry loved Anderson, though for the life of him he could not figure out why. Anderson was his daughter, yes, but she wasn't a nice person. Hadn't been for a very long time before Gentry had come along and said he loved her.

Baldwin had hated that he couldn't control either of them, and that was what pissed him off more than anything. Not once did they come running to him when he tried to bring them down behind their backs, nor did his daughter heel when he told her too. No, Gentry had turned into a good guy, and he was sure that was what had gotten his little girl killed that night. Bart, for all his undying love of his mother, had killed her as surely as if he'd pulled the trigger himself.

Baldwin often wondered what sort of hold he had over her. Bart would have one too. He could dig deeper into someone's life than the men working for him could. That wouldn't be the only reason that Anderson was killed. No, she had made as many enemies as he had. But it mattered little. Bart and Emma had had their own mother killed, and that had sort of been the icing on the cake for him.

"Find out where he lives." Steward handed him something else. He looked it over, all the addresses for the entire bunch of them. "Good. Send someone to the mother's house. There will be a gathering, no doubt, if we put the squeeze on her. And by the way, any word on that ring? Have you found it yet?"

"No. I have men working, sifting through every scrap of material that we can find. There is little doubt he would have taken the ring there. The safe was in the lower levels." He asked him if he thought Emma had taken it. "She more than likely did. But she's not done anything with it as yet. I've never seen the ring, but its value would surely make it worthy of someone speaking about it."

"Yes. I've never seen it either. That fuck really messed things up for me. I had a buyer all lined up, and you can imagine how much I hate to not collect when it is no fault of my own." Steward knew as well as he did that Baldwin had no use for extra money. But he did like having it and lording it over those that didn't. As far as he knew, he was one of, if not the, richest man in the state, perhaps even the whole United States. "She'd better still have it on her, that's all I can say. If not, I'm going to get whoever she sold it to out of her and then kill them too."

After Steward left him, Baldwin picked up the letter and stared at it. He knew that McCade was a good man. When he'd started looking for his wayward granddaughter, he just knew that was where she'd be. The man was just too nice not to help someone in need.

"Going to get you killed too." As he worked on some paperwork, really just wasting time until he had to leave for home, he thought of his daughter again. Anderson had been his baby, the one he was going to leave it all to, he'd thought. She did what he said when he said it and never asked him questions. Then she'd turned fourteen.

He still to this day had no idea what had turned her around. She'd not been what one would call polite. She could be mouthy when the mood struck her. And bitchy too. But she listened to him when he spoke and that was the end of it. Then one day, he noticed that not only had he lost control of her, he wasn't really sure he hadn't been played all along. She talked back to him, slapped around the people that worked for them, and was drunk by two in the afternoon, or sometimes stoned out of her head. Putting her in rehab got to be a monthly thing, and then she'd met Gentry.

Gentry had been a small-time hood. He didn't sell drugs or women which, he supposed had made him small time. If it gave him green, it was a go for Baldwin. But not for Gentry. He did deal with loan sharking, but then who didn't? Broke a few legs too, and had even made an example of a few people. It was one of the reasons that had made Baldwin give the okay for his daughter to marry the younger man. In his opinion, the man was prime meat for working for him. Then he'd gotten his daughter knocked up not six months after they said their vows. Baldwin did not want to be a grandfather.

"Children can change a man." Baldwin nodded at Gentry when he'd told him he was going straight, knowing that the man was full of shit if he thought he was going to allow that. But then his daughter had come to him a few weeks later telling him the same thing. They were out. No more deeds that were going to put either of them in danger. Well, fuck that shit.

But no matter what he'd done to them, either of them, they were set on being just a couple of people making it in the world. No amount of threats, stealing from them, or even telling them that he'd never bail them out if they were ever caught being small time would sway them. They would take it as it came.

Baldwin had recruited Bart almost as soon as the kid was old enough to point and fire a gun. Turning him against his father and mother had been easy. Bart had high tastes and also a taste for drugs. He was almost too easy to get to work for him. Then a few years ago, he'd approached the boy about his father.

"I want you to kill your father." Bart had told him he would. No hesitation either. "You heard me? I want you to kill him for me."

"Yeah, I heard. I'll do it. He's a pain in my ass anyway. Always going on about how I have to be a better man and shit. Then he had the nerve to cut me off, like I'm a kid or something. Being a man like him don't get me what I want." Baldwin asked his grandson what it was he wanted. "All of it."

He'd liked the kid a great deal after that. He knew that Anderson had had troubles with the boy. But Baldwin thought she should have cut him some slack. He was just a growing man, feeling his own feet right now. After that, Anderson forbade him to see Bart. Nor was he allowed to give him any more money. But neither of those stopped when she said so.

About a month after Bart had come to him with an idea to get his dad out of the picture, Baldwin had gotten a call from him. He'd told him that things were a go. That once his father was out of the way, he wanted to come and live with him. But it never happened. His daughter had been killed, and no matter how often or how harshly he asked him, Bart had always denied knowing a damned thing about it.

"Hit and run my ass." And he had never seen her body either. Cremated. Who did that to another man's daughter? Gentry had had it done not hours after she was gone, even before he could see his little girl. And though they hadn't spoken in nearly five years, seeing her one more time before he'd done it to her would have gone a long way in forgiving the man almost anything.

Baldwin was ready to leave for the day when his phone rang. He nearly didn't answer it, preferring most of the time to have the service simply take care of the calls now. But he picked it up and said his name. The silence at the other end had him thinking he'd waited too long, and he nearly hung up before the person that had called him laughed.

"You know where the ring is, Baldwin? I do. I know just where it is." He asked the caller where. "And what do I get if I tell you the information I have? Money, more than I can spend in two lifetimes? Safety from you for the rest of my natural life? What Baldwin? What will you promise me?"

"I'll murder you and your family if you don't tell me." The laughter again, and he was tempted to hang up but didn't. Whatever this person wanted, Baldwin would promise her. That didn't mean he'd actually do it. "You tell me where it is and I'll give you five hundred thousand dollars. Cash."

"That's a great deal of money for a ring, don't you think? For an ugly ring anyway. Unless of course you know what it really is." Baldwin did. It was why he'd had it taken from the man who had it. "So you do know, do you? I thought as much."

"Who is this and where is my ring?" The person laughed again, and he thought it was a woman. There was something very familiar about her too. "I demand that you tell me your name. And who has my property. You will or so help me, I'll make you regret it for the rest of your short, miserable life."

"I don't do well with demands. And the ring is right under your nose if you cared to look hard enough. Besides, if you know the ring and its story, you also know that it's worthless but to the person who can bring it to life." He started to tell her that he knew who could do that, but she continued. "The dragon is awake now, Baldwin, and you should know that he's coming for you too. I have it on good authority that he's a mean bastard."

"What do you mean, the dragon is awake? There are no such things as dragons." But he wondered about it. Taking a deep breath, he let it out slowly, realizing that he had lost control over his temper for a moment. "You never said who this is. Tell me now and we can work on the arrangements of you giving me my ring."

"I never said I was going to get it for you, Baldwin. I only told you I knew where it was. What fun would it be for me to tell you everything I know?" He wanted to tell her to fuck off, that he'd find it himself, but he knew that after all this time, if the ring had been in the shell of the building it would have been found by now.

"Then what is it you want to tell me? Why are you wasting my time calling me and telling me this? Is it that you don't know and think to extort money from me? It won't work. I eat people like you every day before spitting them out on the pavement and moving on." The laughter pissed him off, and he told her to shut up. "Don't call here again. I don't know how you got this number, but don't you dare call here again."

"It's a gold band with a pair of dragons holding a four carat diamond. Their wings are the setting and the diamond is blue, as blue as the oceans where it came from." Baldwin said nothing. That description could have come from the man he'd taken it from. "When all the jewelry is together, each piece is with their owner, the dragon comes forth, taking those that dared thwart him to their fiery deaths. There is the ring, a necklace, earrings, a brooch, and hair combs. And then there is the torques. Few people know that they exist, do they Baldwin?"

"Who is this? Where did you get that information? She laughed again, and he gripped the phone tighter in his hand, trying for a calm speaking voice. "Listen, I really would like to meet with you. Talk over what you know about this."

"Oh, we'll meet, Baldwin, and soon." He waited for her to say more, and then when she did finally speak, he was afraid. "It's really too bad that you won't live long enough to see it come together. I heard that it's quite the sight to see. Until we see each other again, Baldwin, watch your back. I'm going to come for you."

Putting the phone back in the cradle, he staggered to his chair. He'd been on his way out and wished now that he'd never answered the call. He was sure she might have called him later to talk, but he wouldn't have had to deal with it tonight.

He stared out the darkening window and tried to get his thoughts in order. She knew too much, he kept thinking. She had to die too. But who? Where was she and how did she know? The longer he sat there, the longer his list of unanswered questions became. The one thought that kept circling around to him was: he knew the voice.

Chapter 8

"I don't trust her." Kenton looked over at Emma when she spoke to him. He didn't either, but it was her mom and he wasn't sure how to tell her. "Did you know that she talked to your mom for hours yesterday about stuff? She asked about the ring too."

"Mom is upset that she told her anything. I don't think she likes her very much either." Emma snorted, and he felt his dragon move along his skin. He asked him how he felt about her.

She is most dangerous, I think. And I too do not think she's trustworthy. There is something very sly about her. Emma nodded. *I think she's working with the other man, but there is really no way to know for sure, is there?*

"Other man? You mean the one that hired those people to come and take Kenton?" He told Emma that it was. "Do you know who it is? I mean, I have an idea, but do you know him?"

He is a man that she knows, but I don't know any more than that right now. She had no idea what I was either, other than the original family had had me for a great many years before I was taken. I think...I believe that your mother is working with someone else and that she is trying to get the young miss dead. Kenton said nothing, wondering at the lengths that people would go to just to have something that didn't belong to them. *I believe him to be her lover. There is some connection to her father, but I cannot know it just now.*

"My grandfather." Kenton felt the dragon move along his skin, and he felt comforted by it. He did wonder if Emma felt him as well, and Dragon said that she did but not as profoundly. "He's never been in my life. I mean, maybe when I was younger, but I don't remember him well. I think Bart had a lot to do with him, but I'm not even sure about that. What do you think about what she said about Dad and her looking for me?"

"Why would they not know you were under their nose?" Kenton pulled Emma into his arms and thought about some of the other things that Anderson had said. "What do you think about her father not knowing that she's alive? I don't know why, but I do think that part is true. I think he killed Bart for that very reason, don't you?"

"Yes." She looked around the room before continuing the conversation with him. "Why have you done nothing with this room? It's very...I was going to say empty, but there is this couch. Where is all your stuff?"

He'd brought her to his home last night. After they had dinner with his family, he felt it was time for them to be alone. He wasn't sure what his mom would think about them sleeping together now and he didn't want to ask her. Kenton was a grown man, but she was still and forever would be his mom.

"I'm not here much. I mean, I sleep here a few nights a week, but I've not gotten around to getting any furniture yet." She asked him how long he'd lived here. Kenton felt embarrassment run over him when he answered her. "Two years. I told you, I'm not here much."

"Do you at least have a kitchen? Maybe a refrigerator?" He said that he had both and slapped her gently on the bottom. "I know you have a bed and this couch, which is extremely lumpy by the way. And what else? So you know, this place is sparser than mine was."

It was bad. While he did have a kitchen, there were only the basics in it. Not even a table with a single chair. At least when he'd been in college, he'd had a table with a lawn chair to sit on. He thought there was a microwave but wasn't sure if it was even out of the box, much less plugged in. He did have a mattress, but no bed. It had been too much effort to get him one that he liked, so he never bothered. His clothing, his shirt and pants for work, were supplied by a service, and the little bit of things that he needed drawers for had ended up in numerous baskets all over his room. He was almost ashamed of how little he'd done to the place since he'd moved in.

"Let's go shopping." She looked at him with a cocked brow and he laughed. "No, you have no idea how much we need to. Not only is there no food in the house, but I think that I only have a single towel and nothing here for you to wear. The only reason my mom has some of my clothing is because she never changed any of our rooms after we left home."

"That's just…sad really. Seriously? One towel? What do you do if you have it in the laundry?" Kenton assured her she didn't want to know. "Eww. Gross. I had two towels, neither of them in good shape, but I had a backup. Going to the laundromat was hard when you didn't have a car."

He stood up and sat her on her feet. This was going to be fun. As he dragged her through the house and to the kitchen, she jerked her hand from him when they entered the massive room. He was seeing it through her eyes and knew that she found him lacking.

"This is amazing." He nodded, thinking that he was going to buy every gadget he could see just to fill the place. "Do you have any idea how much fun I can have in this room? Oh, Kenton, please tell me that I can cook for us. And have an herb garden too. Please?"

"You like to cook?" She told him that she loved it. "Then we have to get you whatever you need. In case you didn't notice, I have no desire to be in this room any longer than it was necessary to get a glass or cup of tea."

"You have so much space. And cabinets. Look at all these cabinets." Those too were empty of items that one might find in a household, but she didn't seem to care. "And this refrigerator. Oh my, it's a double wide too. And a stove. Look at it. I could have such fun making cookies and things in here."

"You bake too?" She nodded, her eyes filled with excitement. Going down on his knees before her, he took her hand into his. "Marry me."

He had meant it as a joke, but the moment the words came out of his mouth, he knew that's just what he wanted. He wanted her as his wife. The mother of his children and his companion for the rest of his life.

"You have no idea how much I love you. I've been waiting for you my whole life, and now that you're here, I don't ever want to let you go. And the fact that you cook too is a bonus I never thought I'd have." He kissed her finger, the one that had the dragons on it. "You hold within you all that I am. You know that. But you also hold all that I will ever be. My love, my heart, even my body and soul. I love you, Emma Gentry, more than I have ever thought it possible to love a woman. Will you please marry me?"

"Yes." He looked up at her and could see the tears falling down her cheeks. "On one condition, of course. You let me have this as my domain. I have always wanted a kitchen like this. If you just let me have this one room, I will never ask you for anything again. Unless it's more cooking things."

"Deal." Standing up, he kissed her. He loved her. And unbelievably, she loved him too. Backing from her when he realized he wanted to take her right there, he told her they had to fill the house. "In order to sleep here, we're going to need more than a ten year old mattress. I think it was my old one when I went to college. And a few more towels."

He was moving out the door with her as he made a list both verbally and mentally. Christ, it was going to take them all day just to get things for the kitchen. He stopped as they made their way to the car and turned to look at her. He wondered how they were going to buy things and keep her safe, then realized that people like the ones that were chasing her would never think to go to the kind of shops he had in mind. Plus, with his money, Kenton was pretty sure that they could close down the store and have it all to themselves. He was going to do just that. Anything to make her safe.

"Car. You need a car. You can drive, right?" She nodded and laughed at him. "This is very serious. You need a car in the event that I need you to come to my offices and let me fuck you on my desk. Then there is the added advantage that you can go to the store and get whatever you need to cook with, so long as you're careful and take one of us with you. You can cook whatever you want for me and I will love it."

"I like the way you think, Dr. McCade." She got into the passenger side and him under the wheel. As soon as he started the engine, he realized something. "What is it?"

"I have not one clue where to buy furniture at. I mean, clothing at the mall, sure, but where do you buy furniture for a whole house? And I'm sure that mattresses have some specialty store as well." She was still laughing when he called his mom. "Can you tell me where you got that couch in the living room?"

"Oh Kenton, you lovely child. I'm guessing that you're buying furniture. Thank goodness. I'm downtown now. You take me to lunch and I'll show you where to go." He agreed and told her that he had Emma with him. "Well of course you do. Why would you leave her at home when you're buying things for the two of you? Kenton, where is your head today?"

"Fuddled I guess. And she agreed to marry me, so you know." When his mother didn't speak, he thought she was upset. "I love her and I need to spend the rest of my life with her."

"Kenton, that's the most wonderful...I'm sobbing like a little old woman here and people are staring. Come to the Mason Store on Fifth and we'll celebrate with me buying you a lovely living room set." Kenton told her she was neither old nor little. "I love you, son, but you have no idea how long I've thought of you and the others getting married. Now hurry so I can hug you both."

Mason's was a huge seven floor building that had it all under one roof, or so they said on the marquee out front. Beds and linens were on one floor, living room stuff on another. And everything in between spread out all over the place. By the time they'd made it to the top floors, he was sure that he had sat on, picked up, and touched every item in the place once if not twice. But he'd had the most fun on the third floor where the kitchen appliances and silverware were.

Kenton could tell that she wanted it all. Every whisk, all the knives, as well as the pots and pans that hung over the huge old looking butcher block. He asked dragon what she was doing by just moving from piece to piece.

She does not want to overspend. He asked him what that meant. *She has been without for so long, her brother taking what was not his when he robbed her of her pretty things that she knew she could never afford again. She does not want you to think her greedy.*

Greedy? Her? He doubted that she'd ever be that. But he did understand. He moved up behind her and wrapped his arms around her waist as she looked at a set of dining plates. They were pretty, but he had no idea what she liked.

"You'll need to get at least fourteen place settings of whatever you like." She turned in his arms, and he could see that she was upset. "Did someone say something to you? Tell me who and I'll kick their ass."

"No one said…what are you…? You know, I don't care. This place setting is a lot. I mean, just one set is over fifty dollars. Fourteen sets of it is seven hundred dollars. Then there are the things that go with it. Platters, salt and pepper shakers. Even things like bowls to serve in and—"

He put his hand over her mouth. "I have money. Not an endless supply of it, but I haven't spent much since becoming a doctor. I mean, you did have a look around my house, so you know that I'm not one to spend my money needlessly. I inherited my house from my grandfather, so I saved money there. I have no gardener either. I think the kid down the block mows my lawn for a couple hundred bucks a month, but he does a good job and I don't have to mess with it." He picked up the plate and could see him eating from it with his family. "I love this. I can see it stacked nicely in the cabinets just waiting for someone to come and visit us."

"You have built in china cabinets that this will be in if we get it, as you well know. And I'm betting not only do you know the kid's name down the block who mows your lawn, but that you overpay him each time because his family needs the money." He nodded at her. "If I pick this out, this design, you have to pick out the everyday wear, all right?"

He started to ask her if they could just use these, they were pretty, but he saw his mom shaking her head at him. Instead of asking her what she was talking about, he looked at what she had in her hand. It was a plate that had dragons on it. Not well designed ones, but he loved it. Telling Emma yes, he moved to pick up the plate his mom had sat down and moved from and showed it to Emma. She squealed in delight. They had plates now. And everything else that was needed to fill a home was easy after that. Kenton even convinced her that she needed to get all new dishtowels to match the plates, as he was sure that he only had a couple of those as well. Kenton didn't even care what it all cost them. She was happy and that made him happier than he'd ever thought possible.

As they made their way home, after having dinner with his mom, Emma napped lightly in the seat next to him and he wondered how pissed she was going to be about the purchase that Lewis had helped him make without her knowledge. He really did need for her to have a car. He wasn't sure what she was going to do with the big SUV, but he'd gotten it for her and it was at their home. Their home. It sounded so lovely.

~~~

Anderson sat at her husband's desk and surveyed her new home. And it would be hers too, once she found the fucking will. She was sure that he'd left her everything. It was just a matter of figuring out who the attorney was and having things put into order so she could claim it all. The fact that Emma was still alive and around didn't bother her overly much. As far as Anderson was concerned, she was as good as dead.

She was still pissed that her men hadn't been able to kill them all when they'd been cornered in that office. Anderson had a feeling that her father had done that, but when it looked to her like her men were going to be killed instead of the McCades, she'd stepped in and made herself the hero. And she was glad that had fallen into her lap as well. Anderson liked when people thought she was a good person.

Bartholomew hadn't really known where Emma was when she'd come back to him, and he more than likely thought she was dead too. By Bart's hand no doubt. And Anderson wanted him to think that. Having no one to share the wealth with, she thought again, was just fine by her.

When the phone rang, she let it go. No one, as far as she knew, was aware of where she was, so she was sure it wasn't for her. Getting up, she went to the large safe that hadn't been here the last time she'd been in the house. Walking around it again, she wondered what the hell was in it and why Bartholomew had never mentioned getting it.

"What were you thinking?" Walking around the heavy steel box for the third time, she tried to think what he might have done with the combination. She was sure it was going to be something simple, like their wedding day or her birthday. But so far none of those had worked. She'd even tried to use the date she'd "died," and then the one that she'd come back to him, but neither of those were it either. "Who were you trying to keep out of this? Not me, surely. We loved each other, right?"

Anderson laughed. No, she'd not loved her husband, not since he'd told her that going straight was going to be the only way they would live. She'd tried it and had hated every second of it. But he'd said no, and Anderson hated that word as much as she did her daughter and son.

Anderson had come back to her husband of thirty years four years ago. The story that she'd told him was that she'd been in a state of flux, not knowing her name or where she'd come from. Wandering the state, she'd only just gotten her memory back and thought it a good idea that she remain hidden away for insurance, as well as someone possibly coming back to finish the job. It had been a glorious and wonderfully profitable few years with him. At least for her it had been.

Lying to the man had never been so easy. He was so in love with her that she'd been able to get him to do anything she wanted. To a point. And the fact that he didn't want to do them made it so that she was the one getting all the profits instead of sharing them with him.

He still held onto his beliefs that there should be no drugs or drug paraphernalia and no prostitution in his businesses. Stupid when you thought of all the cash he could have had. Or in this case, she had. But he'd been a firm believer that what they had was enough. Enough money, enough cars, as well as enough love to see them through any ups and downs.

"Well, you were wrong about that. I needed what you weren't giving me, and now you have gone and put something here that I can't get into. Why would you think you needed this safe? And why didn't you tell me about it?" She touched her fingers to the key pad and tried just pushing random numbers. Nothing was working. "Damn it, Bartholomew, you were supposed to trust me."

The phone rang again. She was ready to pull the thing from the wall and be done with it when Steward came in the room with her. He was grinning, which made her think that her little phone call to Daddy had worked. He flopped down on the chair behind the desk where she'd been only moments ago, and she wanted to tell him to get up. Christ, the man was making her fucking nuts.

"He is so fucking freaked out right now. Telling me that he knew the voice but not from where. And so you know, Emma and that McCade man applied for a wedding license today. They're set to be married on Friday according to the paperwork. I've already set up a little party for them. They should be married and dead all within an hour of saying their nuptials." He asked her about the safe.

"I don't know. It was here when I got here last night. And according to the bills I found on the desk, it's been ordered and here for a couple of weeks. Long enough for him to have told me, don't you think?" Steward asked her if the combination was with it. "Not that I can find. And according to the billing, they told him how to set the numbers, but they don't know it. The company who sold it, I mean. I even called them and asked. They don't have a way to open it either. I guess that he was going to tell me but never got around to it. Do you have any idea what might be inside this thing?"

"Plenty, I'm betting. I'm sure there are ways to get it opened without the combo." He moved toward it. "It's fucking huge, isn't it? I mean, you could store a body or two in this thing. Whatever is in it, he must have thought he'd be adding a lot of shit to it."

"I have no clue. Anyway, what did you find out about Daddy's will? Did he change it at any time after I was killed?" She wanted to make sure that her dad's money was hers, and Steward had kept assuring her that once he changed it, he'd let her know. But it had been years, and she was beginning to worry that he was holding out on her. "You'd tell me if he changed it, right? I mean anything in it? We can't live without that money, and Bartholomew's will only hold us for a little while, you know?"

"I don't even want to have to think about just living on what your husband might have left you. You said he was frugal, didn't you? And no, your father has not made any changes to his will. He never even asks me about it anymore. Like he thinks he's going to live forever." Not fucking likely. Not with the plans she had for him. "Have you got any more calls to him planned? I'd really like to be there when you call him the next time."

Steward came toward her and slipped his hands up under her blouse. He fondled her breasts for several minutes while she leaned back into his body, hoping that this would be enough for him. She hated sex with him; he was too quick for her needs, and he had the smallest dick she'd ever seen. But he was going to help her get what she wanted, and Anderson wanted it all. So she could live with a little dissatisfaction for now.

"I want to fuck you on your husband's desk again. Take you like you were meant to be taken. Hard and cruelly." He'd done that to her before and she'd walked away with a bruised hip and no relief. But if she didn't give him what he wanted, he would pout for the rest of the day, and she had work to get done. "Lean over it, baby."

She did as he asked and felt him pull her panties off. He had torn them from her the last time, and she'd slapped him. There was no way that he'd do that again, she thought with a small grin. They were expensive, she told him, and she was not going to run around panty-less because he was a jerk.

When her panties were down to her knees, he entered her pussy. No foreplay, no seeing to it that she was wet, he just slammed his tiny dick in her and expected her to enjoy it. Well, she didn't. But then as small as he was, there wasn't much discomfort either.

She was sure that he was enjoying himself. His grunts and groans were enough to make her want to tell him to just get it over with. Moaning a little to help hurry him along, she was thrilled when he shouted to her that he was coming and she pretended, not too much though, that she was as well. When he leaned over her, all Anderson could think of was: Really? That's it? Ten seconds of fucking and he was just worn out.

The phone ringing saved her from having to knock him off her so she could move. When he asked her who it was, it was on the tip of her tongue to tell him that she wasn't a mind reader, but he walked to the desk and looked at the phone himself.

"It says Parker. Do you know him?" Anderson said that she had no idea, and was surprised when he pulled out a sheet of paper and wrote the name and number down. "I have this awesome little app on my phone that allows me to reverse numbers to see who they are."

"Why do you care? A man is calling a dead man?" Steward only nodded at her and smiled that stupid smile that told her that he thought she was just too simple to understand. Anderson could gladly kill him right now. But she needed him, at least for a while longer. "Whatever you want to do, honey. But I have work to do. Convincing my long lost daughter that I have her best interests at heart is hard work. She doesn't seem to trust me."

"Well, that sucks. You're her mother, after all." She was, and somewhere along the line she thought Emma had forgotten that. Like yesterday when she'd asked her about her living arrangements. Wouldn't a mother want to visit her daughter's new home?

"I don't know where we're living right now. My place is too dangerous." It was. Anderson's dad had several people watching the place all day and night. "I know we can't stay here, but I don't have an address as yet."

"You'll move in with Kenton, right?" Emma only shrugged. "Come on, Emma. Why are you not asking him these things? Doesn't he know that you need a place to call your own?"

"I have a place to call mine. I just can't get to it right now." Anderson had seriously thought of burning her old place down, but it would be next to impossible to get close enough to do it. There had to be some way to get her daughter alone. "Where are you staying?"

The question had caught her off guard. Anderson had a sudden thought that Emma knew just where she was living and with who. But she had to think quickly so as not to look like a money grubbing whore, as her daddy had called her once long ago.

Where was she staying indeed? She'd been staying at her own house, one that Bartholomew had bought for her, but now she was in his home. But she thought it not the time to tell her daughter that. Instead, she skipped the question much like Emma did when she'd asked. And now here she was no closer to getting Emma where she wanted her than before.

"Who do you suppose is your husband's attorney?" Steward asked.

She had no idea and hadn't thought to ask him when they'd been together. She had been plotting, keeping him from finding Emma, and making sure he was too busy to notice what she was doing behind his back.

"Why do you care?" He told her. "So you think that he might have not left me the money? Who else would he have left it to if not me? And don't tell me that he thought I was dead. We both know that he's known that wasn't true for years. He might have left some to Bart, but as you know, he's dead as well. And Bartholomew knew that Emma was gone too. Or so I let him believe all these years."

"I don't know what he thought. He was an enigma to me. Still is, actually. He had high standards, as well as a moral set of rules that even most bad guys would admire." Anderson asked him why he thought that was important. "Because, my dear lady, he might have had more up his sleeve than you did. And until the will is read, which won't happen until they find Emma, there won't be any way for us to know."

"What do you mean until Emma is found? You and I both know where she is." Steward sat down on the chair she'd been in when he'd come in. "Don't be coy, Steward. What do you think you know?"

"There is an all-out search for her. Not just your father, but there are two firms that I know of that are seeking information about her whereabouts. Both of which are expensive and highly thought of. I just wonder, and this is why I want to know your husband's attorney, if they are looking for her to open his will up. You certainly can't go and claim it."

"Because I'm dead." He nodded. "Perhaps I can say he told me he left me something, under the name I've been using since I came back."

"Won't work unless you're named in the will. They'll just tell you to wait until they find all the parties that they know are living and go from there." She flopped down on the couch. "Being dead in the eyes of the law is going to fuck you up, my dear."

Anderson was beginning to see that. But she still had to work on getting Emma. She was going to be her ticket to a great many things. And get her back in with her dad. Before she killed them both. Her daughter, then her dad. It was going to be epic.

Chapter 9

"Don't." Emma moved slowly toward the man that was standing near the doorway and put the gun to his head. She didn't know him, he had no badge stating he was with the moving crew, and there was no one near her to confirm or deny who he was. When he put his hands up, she asked him who he was.

"I'm Douglas Parker. I work for…used to work for your father. I was his attorney. I'm going to reach into my jacket pocket and pull out my business cards and identification." Before he moved, she poked the gun harder into his head. "Or not. You have to believe I'm who I say."

"No, I don't. What I have to do is protect myself from idiots that can have business cards printed up for ten bucks for a thousand. Not to mention, you're not wearing a suit. Don't all you lawyerly types wear suits?" He laughed and told her she was most assuredly her father's daughter. "That's not really helping you much, Mr. Parker."

"You're not to trust your mother." She told him she didn't trust anyone. "Good girl. Your father left you a letter. He didn't know when he was going to be killed, but he figured his days were numbered. He had cancer. Did you know that?"

"I knew nothing about him other than what my brother and now my mother told me." Douglas nodded but still hadn't moved. "Why should I not trust my mother? Not that I don't believe you, but you have to have a reason."

"I do. May I turn around please? I'd like to see if you're as pretty as your father said you were." The dragon told her to trust the man, that he could tell he wasn't lying. So she told the man he could turn. "You are. Much prettier than he said."

"Fuck off." Douglas nodded and asked her where Kenton was. "Why do you want to know? If you hurt him or this family, I will kill you where you stand and put you in the back yard for the wolves to eat."

"They won't have a thing to do with my carcass. I'm like them." She saw the wolf run along his skin and took a step back. "I won't hurt you. But I would like to see Kenton. He and I are old friends, and he will vouch for me."

"He's delivering a baby at the moment. Jorden is here, as is his other brother, Karl." The man said there was no brother named Karl, but good try. "Okay, so if you're such good friends with him, what is he? And his brothers?"

"Other than the best doctor I've met, you mean? He's a dragon." Her dragon laughed and said that she was most untrusting. She told him to be quiet. "You should really let me reach into my pocket and give you the letter I have for you. It will go a long way to explaining a great many things."

"The police are looking for me. So is someone else, trying to kill me too. How did you find out where I am?" He looked over her shoulder a little and smiled, but she didn't trust him to think he was fooling with her. "I asked you a question."

"Mrs. McCade. You are as lovely as ever." Her future mother-in-law might have been behind her or not, but when she came around her to stand next to Douglas, she lowered her gun. "I was just telling Emma here how pretty she is. I think you might have some competition for my heart."

"Oh, go on with you. You know as well as I do that pretty mate of yours will have me for dinner. And speaking of which, you should come by tomorrow night with your family and join us. It's been too long." They both looked at her as Aisha continued. "Emma, honey, you are smart not to trust this scoundrel. He's been the biggest flirt I know for years."

The man was suddenly gone, as Grady swept him up in a bear hug and took him to the floor. She wasn't sure if they were friends or enemies until Grady laughed. Emma wasn't sure she'd ever get used to these men. They were too...big and friendly sometimes. When both men stood up, Douglas asked if he could reach into his pocket now.

"You have a letter from a man that had no idea where I was when I worked in the same building he did. Why should I care to read it?" He retrieved the letter and held it out to her. She could see her name across the front of the cream-colored envelope and felt her fingers itching to take it. "How did you find me?"

"I'm a wolf and there are wolves on this property. They belong, I guess you could say, to me. I am their alpha. I could find you when the others could not simply because I didn't use conventional ways." He took her hand and wrapped it around the envelope. "Your father had no idea you were working for him until two weeks before his death. It was then that he discovered a great many things. Like the fact that your brother was hurting you and stealing most of your paycheck. Did you know that he was having your checks routed through his account, and you were only getting less than a third of it?"

"He said that Dad didn't want me to have anything because I was a girl and not the son. And when I tried to see him, I was cut off, told he didn't want to see me." Douglas told her that was the fault of her mother. "She knew where I was as well?"

"Oh yes. She liked having you there, we think. I was never sure if she and Bart were in on it together, but I think not. And when your dad found out about it, he was livid. But he needed more time, more information before he could confront either of them, your mother or your brother." Emma moved to what they'd called the parlor and asked him to have a seat. Jorden joined them then, telling her and Douglas that Kenton was still in surgery, and he wanted him to make sure that Emma was all right. "He wanted to bring you home, take care of you the way he thought you should be. But, like I said, there were things going on that he needed to take care of so that you'd not get hurt in the crossfire."

"What did he think had happened to me? And if it's all the same to you, I'll read this when Kenton is here with me." Douglas told her that was fine. He was brought his briefcase by one of the new staff, a man that all the brothers knew. "Why are you here? I mean, other than this letter; you could have mailed it to me."

"I could have, I suppose, but I have other things that he wanted you to have. Like I said, his days were numbered, and if you want the truth, going the way he did was more than likely less painful." Her heart broke for her father, a man she barely knew. "In answer to your question, he thought that you'd been killed. Not right after you left home for your own job, but right after your mother was…killed. Then things started popping up that made him believe that you were alive. Most of which was that no one claimed to have killed you. And a man like him, he was sure that if someone had killed you, they would have bragged."

She could see that, she supposed. "So he figures out I'm alive, yet leaves me to be the punching bag to my brother, who he loved more than anything."

"No, he didn't care for Bart at all. In fact, he hated him almost as much as Bart did him. Bart was about to be moved out, so to speak. And so you know, he was only your half-brother. Your mother had an affair just after they were married, and Bart was the result. We were made aware of that a few weeks ago too." Emma had wondered about that. Bart didn't look like her dad and not even her mom really, but she said nothing to Douglas. "There is a will. It was made out three weeks ago. Changes were made to it that made you the sole heir to all of his holdings. The insurance policy on your mother, the one he could have collected when she was declared dead, has never been cashed in, so there won't be any penalties on that either. He committed no fraud in that."

"You're saying this as if I might want that money." She looked over at Jorden when he cleared his throat. "You think I should take it?"

"It's up to you. But I would like to point out that you have no idea what he was thinking when he did that, so I'd hold judgement on that for now. You might be surprised to figure out that he had his reasons and that they were good ones." Emma said he could have helped her when he was alive. "True, but had he acknowledged you in any way, I think you'd be dead now and not with Kenton. He might have saved your life."

Emma said nothing but looked at the sealed envelope again. It would tell her a great deal, and it also might tell her nothing at all. It was why she wanted Kenton to be there for her. When Douglas said her name, she looked at him, feeling lost and scared, like she was ten again.

"You are the only person named in the will that is to receive anything from him. Bart was mentioned, but that is a moot point now. And so is your mother. But she gets nothing. I would very much like to read it to you now." She started to shake her head. "Even if Kenton were here with you, Emma, he can't be a witness. You're not married. I have brought my assistant with me, and he's going to act as the second party to this. If you'll allow me, I want to do this for your father. He was a good man, despite being a fool where Anderson was concerned."

She told him to go ahead and do it then. A man by the name of Sherwood James was brought in and he had her sign off on what was about to happen. When Douglas opened the one page document, she wanted to ask him if there was so little, but he started to read it and she had to hold onto the chair arms to get a grip. After reading the beginning, stating his name and address, her father's words flowed over her.

"To my only child, Emma Anderson Gentry, I leave the vast holding of my personal and business assets. This will include but not single out any holdings that are in the process of being purchased or any sales of said properties that are in the process of being closed. Any monies from said sales or purchases are also hers to do with as she pleases."

Emma stopped Douglas to ask him what that meant. "Your father was in the process of buying out two companies that he thought that he could make work, as well as several buildings downtown that have now been added to the estate. There is a home here too that is included with the others. I believe that he bought it for your mother to live in, but has since changed his mind on giving it over to her in his will."

"And I can sell it if I wish. No one can stop me." He said that it was hers to do with as she pleased. "I see. And my mother, what will she think about this will? I'm assuming that she doesn't know about it."

"She does not. Nor does she know about me. Not that it was ever any of her business, but your father and I conducted business alone and without her knowledge, especially about you and this will, in private." She nodded. "You should also be aware, and I don't want you to be surprised by this, but this will was executed before your brother died. He is mentioned here, as I said, but there is no one to contest this will. You will be a very wealthy woman, and no one can ever take it from you." She told him to go on.

When Douglas got to the part where he mentioned Bart and her mother, she could understand the bitterness of his actions. They had both hurt him, more than they had by keeping the two of them apart. Her father started on her mother.

"To Anderson Frank Gentry, mother of my daughter, I leave nothing. I do not wish her to be present during the reading of this will, for I do not wish to subject my daughter to her drama. Or her violence. It has occurred to me that she may wish to harm my child, and I have taken steps to make sure she is aware of this will's contents in private. She will be notified at a later time of what I have said here."

"To Bartholomew Baldwin Gentry, I leave the DNA tests that were taken on September 9th of this year." At this point Douglas told her that it was actually last year, but the paperwork would show that. Nodding, she listened as he continued. "You are no son of mine, as the tests will show. I also have proof that you were aware of this, long before I was, and had kept that information to yourself for your own personal gain. It is my wish that you get nothing from me, as I have paid dearly for this lie that has been told to me over and over."

She was still sitting in the parlor later when Kenton came home. He might have been sitting in front of her for a little while, but she looked at him when he took her hands into his. She moved across the couch to sit in his lap and told him to hold her.

"You're all right now, love. I have you." She nodded, holding him to her even as the tears started to fall. "What happened? Jorden told me that you've been in here for hours, and he was worried about you. I came home as soon as Mrs. Bailer had her twins."

It was too much. Everything seemed to hit her at once. The building blowing up. The ring that had a dragon in it. Her brother not being her father's child. Her mom not being dead. It was rolling around in her head like a string of bad horror movies, and she needed a reprieve.

"I have to bake something." She got up off his lap and made her way to the kitchen, knowing that he'd follow her. She started pulling out ingredients for pumpkin pecan cobbler. "You know that this attorney guy came by, I guess. He gave me a letter from my dad. Oh, and can we get married soon? I don't like not having you around when crap like this goes on."

"All right. What did the letter say?" She told him that she hadn't read it yet. "And you were hoping for me to read it for you? I don't understand why you'd not want to know what he had to say."

"I do. Just not with strangers around." She started measuring the ingredients into a large mixing bowl. She'd been wanting one of these cobblers for months now, and when they'd gone grocery shopping she'd picked up what they would need. "Douglas said that my father knew where I was but was afraid to show me that for fear of me being killed. He didn't trust my mother either, apparently. And we're rich."

"We are. Do you want me to go and get the letter for you?" She turned to look at him, knowing that he was misunderstanding her. She let it go, then nodded for him to get the letter. While he was gone, Dragon spoke to her.

Another part of me has been found. I wanted to tell you that so that you could be prepared. She asked him what she had to be prepared for. *When I am touched by the one that brings me here, you will feel it too.*

Feel what? Emma wasn't surprised to hear Kenton's voice in her head as well, and waited for an answer from the dragon.

Power. When Kenton entered the kitchen with her again, she turned to look at him. Power? They were going to feel power? How the hell did one feel power?

Before she could ask him about it, even if she was sure she wanted to know, she put the cobbler in the oven, then started on dinner. Some things, she decided, were better left for later. The laughter in her head made her think that Dragon didn't think so. But for now, she was fine with it.

~~~

Baldwin wondered where everyone was. He'd been there for nearly ten minutes and not one person, from his cleaning crew to his staff, had shown up. He glanced at his watch again and saw that it was well after eight o'clock, well past time for the workday to begin.

He was just reaching for the phone to call Steward when he came into the room. Sauntered was more like it, but he sat down and smiled at him, and Baldwin thought that perhaps when this was all done, he'd have to lay the man out tied to a table and pull every one of his pearly white teeth out with a pair of pliers.

"I have wonderful news." Baldwin didn't ask. He wanted to but was too pissed right now to give in. "I know where she is."

"Who?" He knew just who he was talking about and didn't have to work as hard as he'd thought to make himself look bored with him. "You lost someone?"

Frustration. It was a beautiful sight on someone else's face for a change. When Steward started to reach for his briefcase, Baldwin wanted to ask him if he ever didn't have to refer to it when he had information. And why did he have to hand him files every time too? It was annoying as fuck.

"Your granddaughter and the McCade man have applied for a marriage license. The day of the nuptials is Friday at the courthouse." Baldwin nodded. He'd known this. Yesterday, as a matter of fact. As he was handed the file, the fucking file, he got a whiff of the man's cologne. Or, what he thought was his cologne for all of a second, when what it really was hit him.

Memories flooded his mind. His daughter's first steps. The day that she'd gotten on the bus to go to kindergarten.

The day she'd gone to the mall alone and had called him in a panic when her credit card hadn't worked. The day he'd gotten the call from her that she'd been killed. He looked at Steward and realized that the man was looking at him oddly. Baldwin took the file and laid it on his desk and let his mind work.

As the man prattled on about whatever his head had to empty out, Baldwin tried to think if someone had gotten into Anderson's room and given her things away. That was the only reason in the world that he could think that Steward would have on her perfume. A perfume that he'd made especially for her and had shipped to her for her sixteenth birthday. He would have to make a few calls to find out what the hell was going on.

"Baldwin?" He looked at Steward and realized that he'd missed something. "I was asking if you want someone to be there to get her then. We'll know just where she's going to be."

"Yes. That's a good idea. Yes. I like it." He wanted Steward out, not just out of his sight but gone for good. Whatever was going on, he knew that this man was in on it. "When did you say it was again? And where? I might just show up to watch the proceedings myself."

"Friday, at the courthouse. There is family—his is pretty extended—and friends. The reception will be at their home later. I have that address in the file for you. It's at four in the afternoon. But with my plans, they'll never make it to that."

Nodding, he told Steward he had a lot of work to do and ushered him out with the promise that if anything changed, he was to be informed. As soon as he was gone, Baldwin pulled out his ledger.

Finding the number was harder than he thought it should have been, but then Steward did this kind of work for him usually. Today, though, he needed to know what the other man was up to. Something was off. Baldwin wasn't sure what it might be, he just wanted answers. Calling the man who had helped him create and make Anderson's signature perfume gave him some answers, but opened a lot more questions.

"I am sorry, sir, but I have done as you asked and have given this to no one but your daughter. She is the only one, besides you that is, that has the code." The tag number on the perfume that was simply called Anderson. "I will check when the last shipment was sent out. I know that it was recent."

Recent. For a man as old as Toby had been back then, it could have been a decade ago. But the longer he sat there waiting for him to get his information, the more he thought the man was right. It had been recent. And Baldwin had a feeling that not only did Steward know where his daughter was, but that he was fucking her too.

When Toby came back and confirmed his worst thoughts, he told the man that he was glad that it was working out for him. He assured him that it was a pleasure to have been able to speak to his daughter after so long.

"She is still just as bossy as she was as a youngster, is she not? Telling me that there was a new billing address for the shipment and that the address was new as well. I did as she asked, for she has been a good customer, and I love working with you as well, sir. You tell her that it will be a pleasure to continue to work with her." Baldwin asked him for the address, saying that he wanted to make sure that it was the one he had. "Yes, I can understand that. It's good that you care for her so much."

His daughter was alive, and ordering perfume as if nothing had happened. He put the phone in the cradle, sure the man was still talking as what was going on started to form in his head. Anderson was fucking with him. And so was Steward.

Now what to do. He'd been devoting his entire life for the last years, since he'd gotten that call, in avenging her death. And now here she was, not only alive but acting as if nothing had happened. And she'd not contacted him. In any way. Did she not think he'd want to...? He leaned back in his chair.

Had Bartholomew known? Of course he had. The perfume was going to that house, and had been for a while now. Did the kids know? Bart more than likely did not know. Had he, then Baldwin was sure he would have said something...a slip of the tongue. Steward knew, and that was going to get him killed. And he was positive for some reason that Emma didn't. This was something that bore looking into, much deeper than he had before.

"Heads are going to fucking roll, that's for sure." He picked up his pen and the file that Steward had given him, and decided that he needed to make his own plans. Beginning with a list. "Why did she fuck with me?" headed the top of this one.

Chapter 10

The courthouse was filled with people. Some Emma knew, most she didn't. She was surprised by that. No one but the family was supposed to attend, yet there were enough people in the little room to fill a large hall. Emma looked at Aisha when she touched her fingers to her cheek.

"You were so far away. Do you not want to marry Kenton?" Emma told her what she was thinking and that she wanted that more than anything. "Yes, most of them are friends of the family, but a lot of them are here in the event that we have unwelcome guests. They can be such a bore, don't you think? Kenton and the others, they'll keep you safe."

"You mean from the people trying to kill me?" Aisha nodded and smiled. "I thought this was going to be just a few people. We say I do and go on with our lives the way it has been. Maybe a little less stressful but, you know, onward."

"I would imagine that some of this stress, as you call it, will go away in due time. But for now, it's what we're dealing with and we'll do well." Emma thought the woman was just too calm and asked her why. "I'm gaining a daughter today. Perhaps grandchildren, too, out of this. And Kenton is happy. That in and of itself has me thrilled beyond words. He loves you very much. And, believe it or not, I've fallen in love with you as well. You are a treasure to us all, Emma."

"Thank you for that. I love you as well. All of my new family." Emma looked down at the dress she had on. It wasn't white, nor was it the most traditional dress she could have worn. But it had made her feel pretty, and she needed that right now. "He and I have a lot of things to work out, you know. I mean…my father left me all his money, and I don't know what to do with it. Or even if I want it."

"I can understand that. He wasn't in your life for a long time, I know that. But he didn't know where you were. And for some reason, I believe that as well. I would imagine that finding you alive and not being able to take you into his arms was difficult for him. It would have been for me." Emma knew that too. Her father, in his way, had kept her alive. And it helped a great deal in dealing with things to know that. "I'm to understand that there is a great deal of money from him, as well as properties."

"Yes. Just over sixty million in money, and almost that much more in lands and holdings. I had no idea that he was that wealthy." Aisha said nothing. "I've made Kenton my partner in all of this. My attorney, Douglas, said that making him a partner is better than just giving him access to all of it. I have no idea why, but that's what we did. He has just as much right to it as I do, and anything that I have, he does as well."

"You are equal, I think is what he was saying to you." Emma said that they were. "And this wedding, the rushing of it, is that what this is about too?"

"No. I mean a little. Because we're not married as yet, Kenton was left out of a lot of things that Douglas wanted to talk to me about. I don't care for that. And I love him. We were going to marry anyway, but this makes it easier on both of us." Aisha nodded and smiled. "Did you know that your sons are afraid of you?"

"Yes. I encourage that. I would hope that you are a little as well, but I doubt you will be. If you want to know the truth, you scare me a little too." Emma asked her why. "The way you handled those men that came to the house. You do know that I was ready to invite them in, right?"

"Yeah. Well, I knew later. Jorden explained about the compulsion and that they were making you do it. I'm learning. Did I tell you that I had a dream about you and those men before it happened? Bart was there as well, and he shot you, I think. Anyway, it wasn't until afterwards that I remembered it. Dragon said that I saved everyone by doing what I did." Aisha asked her what the dragon said about it all. "He has an opinion about everything, I think. But he's right, saving you did make things better for all of us. The dragon, you knew what he was, Kenton said. And that he'd come back someday."

"Yes. I had hoped that it would be in my lifetime, but I wasn't sure. I'm glad, but I have to tell you I'm terrified at the same time. Kenton's dragon is beautiful. You gave him that. But I do worry about what the others will bring with them when they bring the other parts to us." Emma nodded and walked to the window to look out. She was nervous and needed a distraction. "Emma, the other person who is coming, do you suppose she'll be the mate to one of my other sons?"

"I do. I don't know why, but I think that's how it's going to work. Dragon said that the reason that Kenton can't fly is because his wings aren't here yet. I think I understand that each part of him will give each of the men a part of their dragon too. I don't know what piece goes with what power, and Dragon doesn't either, but I'm nervous about that as well."

Emma thought about Kenton's dragon. He'd shifted last night while they were in the yard looking over the property. She'd seen him before, of course, but she thought he was bigger than before, and much stronger.

He was as tall as Kenton was, at just over six foot six. And he was big, muscular like him too. The blue of his body was the same color as the ring she wore, and just as brilliant. Scales seemingly moved along his body, brilliant against the stars that seemed to be as much a part of him as they were the lights above his head. When he moved, his colors seemed to capture parts of the earth, and he would pick up the greens, browns, and any other color around him. It looked to her as if he could fade into them too.

His wings would open, but he couldn't use them, they were told, until it was time. It took them nearly an hour to figure out what time that would be. The dragon, it seemed to Emma, was just as confused about things as they were. But Kenton wrapped her in them. His wings had fit around them both and she felt safe, for the first time in a very long time.

All parts of me have to be brought together. She asked him what that meant. *I'm not sure, my lady. The set of jewels must be here to bring forth that part of me that makes me whole. That much I do know. As for the rest, I have been dormant for so long,*

I am no longer sure of it. I think…I'm not sure, but I think some part of it will bring my wings out and all of you may use them.

"So, of all the pieces that are coming here, you don't have any idea which piece brings what part of you awake? Nor what that means for the rest of us that have our part here already." Dragon told Kenton that he did not. "That's not too terribly helpful. You know that, right?"

"Emma?" Emma turned and looked at Aisha again, bringing her once again to the present. She'd zoned out again and had no idea why she was doing that. "We're ready if you are."

Nodding, she turned away from the window and then back. Someone was there, just beyond the building across from her, and she thought she knew them. But it couldn't be. Why would her grandfather show up here, and seemingly alone, today of all days? She moved to the doors just as they were opened, and she saw Dalton. And he didn't look happy.

"You saw him." He nodded even though she'd not asked. "Did you talk to him? Tell him to get the fuck out of here?"

"He wants to talk to you about something." She nodded, waiting for him to tell her that he told him no. "I think you should listen. If for no other reason than to clear the air. He told me that there is a plan for you to be murdered on your wedding day, and he's glad that you didn't do as you said. He knew that we changed the day to today and not tomorrow."

"You mean he wants to talk to me by him putting a bullet in my head?" She took a slow deep breath when she realized how loud she'd been. "What did he tell you? That he has had a change of heart and now wants to be my best bud?"

"He said that he had no idea that your mother was alive, and that he believes she's sleeping with his assistant. And that she's plotting to have you killed." Emma asked him if everyone wanted her fucking dead. "I don't. Neither does Kenton. Or the rest of my family."

"I don't like you right now." He laughed. "When does he want to see me? If it's all the same to you, I'd just as soon it wasn't right now. I sort of have shit going on."

"I told him that I'd talk to you and Kenton and then we'd set up a place where I'm in charge." Emma nodded, still not at all sure about this. "We'll make sure that he's alone and not armed. And we'll take him to the place from wherever we meet him without his prior knowledge. He won't be able to set things up so that you or the rest of us are ambushed. You can trust me on this: he won't be able to hurt you again."

She wasn't so sure about this, but they signaled for her to come to the judge's chambers. This was the best way, she thought, to get married. No muss no fuss. She knew that Aisha was disappointed, but she agreed that it was safest.

After going to the dais and standing there, she looked around at the people that in a few moments she'd be related to. Emma already loved them. Each of them were friendly, loving, and polite to her. Well, everyone really. Aisha had done a very good job raising her boys, as she called them. Emma had never had a family, or at least one that she had any desire to spend time with. But these men, she thought perhaps she was going to have the best time of her life with them. And was glad that she'd slipped the ring on her finger that day.

Kenton was waiting for her. He looked so good in his suit and tie. She felt her mouth water when she thought of the sexy little nighty that she'd gotten yesterday when shopping for a dress, and wondered what he'd say when he saw her in it. She was sure that it wouldn't be on long, and that was what she was counting on. Smiling at him, she told him that she loved him with all of her heart.

"I love you too. Very much so, and am happy you are marrying me." She smiled at him when he kissed her on the nose. The judge, a very nice man, cleared his throat. Kenton smiled at him as he spoke. "I can't help myself, Your Honor. She's just too pretty not to want to kiss all the time."

"Be that as it may, young man, we have things going on here that require a certain amount of decorum. Now, let's get the two of you hitched up, shall we?"

Twenty-five minutes later she was Mrs. Emma McCade, married to the man she loved more than anyone else. Then, just as they were introduced to the rest of the people in the room, each brother—all five of them— welcomed her to the family by planting a big kiss on her mouth. She'd never been so thoroughly embarrassed in her lifetime.

~~~

Kenton laid his gun on the table just as Baldwin Franks was shown into the room. He didn't care for it, hated having it on his person. But he knew how to use it and would if the man proved to be stupid.

Dalton had searched him, and even the wolf that was one of his police buddies had said that he didn't so much as have a single ounce of steel on him. Not a knife or a screw was found to be a part of his clothing. As he sat down across from him and Emma, the man looked lost.

"I've been a fool. Not that I won't continue to be one, but on this, I've been had as much as you have, I'm afraid." Kenton said nothing, and looked at Emma when Baldwin did. "You look like my mother did when she was younger.

I'm glad for that. Your mother only looked like herself. Not a very good representation of herself either. I think…no, I know that I fucked up royally, and in that, I've lost something very important. But I can fix it…even if it's just a little, I can fix some of this."

"What do you mean by that?" There was censure in her voice when Emma asked her grandda, and when she realized what she'd said, she cleared her throat. Kenton was proud of her in that moment. "I mean, why you think my mother is a fake? I'm assuming that's what you mean."

"It is and she is. I guess I knew that all along, but it was easier to give in than to listen to her lambast me about how she was underprivileged and so on. That part I take on as my own fault. But some of this, I lay it at her door. I guess I knew, way deep in my heart, that she was a terrible person, but I never dreamed the extent of her evilness." Kenton said nothing. He'd seen spoiled children like the man was describing his own daughter as. The difference was, he was ashamed of what he'd done, Kenton thought, rather than proud of what he'd created. "I was told that you were to be married on Friday. I'm assuming that it was always on Thursday afternoon, and that you knew there might be trouble."

"Yes. The courthouse isn't opened on Saturday or we might have done it on that day instead. Whoever told you that was mistaken." Baldwin nodded at him, but Kenton wasn't sure what point he was trying to make. "Did Anderson tell you that we were getting married tomorrow?"

"No. My assistant did. I think, as I told your brother, that Steward is fucking…sleeping with Anderson. And that for some reason, they're plotting your demise. I can't be one hundred percent sure of that, but I think it's as good as done as far as they're concerned. Especially since you're your father's only living relative as far as the courts are concerned, and you stand to inherit all of his money and property. It would be difficult if not impossible for her to inherit since she is supposed to be dead. That would be my guess."

"I did get it all, and we've already been informed of it the other day. My father figured out what was going on before he was killed." Kenton nodded at Emma to continue when she glanced at him. "Bart worked for you. And in doing so, I think he killed my father. You believed that Bart killed my mother, or at least had something to do with her supposed death, didn't you?"

"I did. He did have everything to do with it. And he admitted as much to me when I saw him in the hospital just before he killed himself and that young man with him. He also said that you were in on it, but I've since figured out that he lied about that as well. Bart was very good at blaming others for things he'd done. I should have known that. But I don't think he knew she was alive. Do you?" Kenton had a feeling, like Emma did, that he'd been helpful in Bart's suicide. Emma told her grandfather that she didn't think Bart knew, but had never been sure. "He had a bomb in the sublevels of the basement where you worked too. Did you know that? It was set to go off when the building was empty. It's too bad that all those other people had to die for things to come to light about Bart."

Kenton, like Emma, believed that her grandfather had been a part of that as well. The bomb squad had found the other device, set far enough away from the one that had gone off that it was still intact. Bits and pieces of the other bomb had been found in the wreckage. The one that had killed everyone had been much bigger, as well as set to go off when the building was full, as it had been that day.

"Yes. It's very sad my father was killed senselessly. But I'm to understand that he was nearing the end of his life anyway. He had inoperable cancer, I was told." Kenton wanted to ask Baldwin if he'd done it, but he wasn't sure what they wanted to know. Not really.

"Emma, did you have anything to do with the disappearance of your mother? I know what Bart told me, and I don't believe him. But I needed to ask you." Baldwin looked...broken came to mind. Sad for sure. And Kenton was sure he was angry as well. Men like Baldwin did not like to be thwarted in their plans.

"No, I had nothing to do with her much before her 'death,' and I don't really want her in my life now. As far as I knew, she was dead. And I think my father believed that as well. He mourned her. I think, in his own way, he even loved her. But no, I had nothing to do with it. As I said, I do know that she wasn't the nicest person in the world and she wasn't a very good mother. She and I never got along. She and Bart were close, or so I thought. Did you know that Bart wasn't my father's child?"

Kenton was watching Baldwin's face, and knew that he might have guessed it but didn't know for sure. He asked if Bartholomew had known. Kenton pulled out the letter that Emma's father had given her and handed it to Baldwin. He read it and set it back on the table.

"She ordered her perfume." Kenton started to ask Baldwin what he meant when he continued. "She'd ordered some of her own scent three days after she was supposed to have been killed. The scent that I'd commissioned to be made for her when she was younger. And she sent me the bill. I rarely go over the credit card statements, so I never noticed it. But a few days after she was murdered, an order was placed and sent to an address out of state. I found nine more such charges, not including her rent on the place she was staying and a car rental. It never occurred to me to look for her. I thought she was dead. I went back over my records after I had an encounter with her scent, on Steward. He is playing me for a fool, and I'm going to take care of him."

"She was charging your accounts and you never knew a thing?" Baldwin nodded at Emma, and Kenton could almost feel sorry for him. The man had been hoodwinked as well. "I don't trust her. Nor did my father, it seems. But to be as low as to continue on as if nothing had happened, as if no one was mourning her…. That's about as callus as it comes, don't you think?"

"It's the way she did things. Always. Your father…I never realized what kind of man he was. I mean, not since he was killed. I looked into some other things when I realized that Anderson had played me. I guess she played him as well." Kenton asked him why he'd done that, investigated her dad. "I thought he was a sap, to be honest with you. And had I had my way, Anderson would never have married him. Not for any reasons that you might think. I simply thought she could do better. Come to find out, I think he could have done a hell of a lot better than Anderson. As for Bart not being his child, I'm sorry for that. I knew that she was willful and headstrong, I just never realized how fucking stupid she was too."

"She believes that she'll inherit all of Bartholomew's money." Baldwin told him that he was more than likely right on that score. "But the will was changed, a few days before he was killed. And I know that she's staying at his home with another man. Steward Jefferies. Do you know him?"

"He's my assistant, or he was. He is still under the impression that he is, but I plan to take actions on that as well. Steward told me about the wedding. I'm assuming that you changed it on purpose to today and not Friday." Kenton told him. "You don't trust them either. Good for you. I wonder if they might have had some plans for you and Emma. I'm sure of it if we're being honest."

"I'm sure they might have. But this way, if they show up tomorrow, then they'll meet with some people that will be happy to see them. Even though Bartholomew never cashed in the insurance policy he had on his wife, faking your own death is a crime. And Steward will be held as her accomplice." Baldwin nodded and asked if he could get up and pace. "Sure, but you go to the window for any reason and you'll be dead before you can step away from it again."

Baldwin just stared at him. It was several tense seconds before he laughed. And when he did, Kenton smiled at him. It went a long way in easing some of the tension in the room.

"You think I'd have someone out there that would come in and shoot you full of holes? I love it. At another time I might have…no, I would have done just that. I'm a man who likes things neat and tidy. But so you know, I'm not going to do shit to either of you. And that you can take to the bank. I would, however, like to help you in bringing my daughter down. She's hurt a great many people for long enough." Kenton asked him about the people he'd hurt. "I'm sure that someday I'll pay for that too, but Anderson fucked with the wrong person when she decided to screw around with me and mine."

"And who would you consider yours, Grandda? Me?" Kenton looked at Emma when she spoke. He could feel her pain too, how it hurt her that this man would be willing now, after all this time, to help her out. "I don't want anything from you. You were never willing to love me or show me any love while I was right there for you to see. So having it now, that's not really anything I care to have. It's too little too late."

"It is, and I'm sorry for that. Profoundly so. Had I had more contact with you, I'm not sure you would have liked me any better. But I'll agree with you about my treatment of you. I've been a fool, as I've said. And a bigger fool for believing everything I heard from other people." He nodded to the letter that still lay there. "Your father at least had an excuse. I only wanted you dead for a part that you had no more to do with than anyone else. Anderson was my little girl, and she fucked us both over. For her own personal gain no less. I'm actually ashamed of her."

They talked for another hour. Baldwin was a man used to getting his own way, and no matter how much he tried to tell Emma he would help, she turned him down. Not that Kenton blamed her. She'd been screwed by them all enough. But Kenton could see the determination in the older man's eyes, and wouldn't be surprised to see him taking action against Anderson on his own terms.

"She's to meet us tomorrow at the courthouse." Emma said nothing as Kenton told Baldwin what he knew. "We won't be there, of course, but she won't know that until it's too late. If she shows, and I have no reason to believe that she won't, there will be a few people there waiting for her that have a few hundred questions. You can do what you want with her after if she's free or whenever. But we're going away for the weekend and won't be back until Monday."

They moved out of the building and to the waiting limo. Kenton had had the local hotel reserve them a room with all the trimming befitting a new bride and groom. He wanted this to be as special as they could make it under the circumstances. And later, when this was settled, he was going to take her on a cruise for a month. Kenton wanted it all for his new wife.

When Emma started to enter the room ahead of him, Kenton scooped her up in his arms. He was doing this right.

The room was as beautiful as he'd hoped. Roses in vases were on every flat surface. Petals of the fragrant flowers were spread out over the bed, and a single red bud sat on the middle of the pillows as he had requested. He had had champagne chilled for them, as well as a tray of meats and cheese set out. There was a large basket filled with more fruit, and even another bottle of the sparkly wine from his family, and a note from them telling them both to love each other but to keep up their strength too. He thought that Lewis had put the card together.

"You're such a romantic." He nuzzled her neck and then nipped at her creamy flesh. "Kenton, you're making me nuts doing this. Put me down so I can show you what I bought you."

He held onto her, pulling her tighter to his chest and heart. He loved her. Kenton had told her that before, but seeing her with her grandda and hearing him talk about the love lost, Kenton knew he was a very lucky man.

"If you think you're getting out of my sight, you're sadly mistaken." He sat her on her feet and pulled her body to his. "I love the way you smell right now. All fresh and sexy."

"How does one smell sexy, I wonder? But then I think you smell that good too. Did I tell you that I have a wonderful nighty?" His cock, already hard as stone, seemed to thicken and make his pants even tighter as her words registered in his head. "It's blue like you are when you're my dragon, and very see-through as well. Very lacy. I've been thinking about it all day and what you'd think when you saw it on me. You do want to see me in it, don't you?"

He took a step back from her, and she giggled. "If you want to be able to go put it on, I would suggest that you go now. Run, as a matter of fact." When she didn't move, he reached for her again, and then she took a step back. "Emma, I'm holding on by a very thin thread right now. Go and make me beg."

"Oh Kenton, I plan to make you beg. All night long." As she moved by him, lifting up his tie and pulling him close enough for a kiss, he thought he was going to die. She was his wife, all his, and she was going to kill him.

Laughing, he pulled off his tie and jacket. Pulling the bottle out of the ice, he poured her a glass and then himself one. As he undressed, slipping out of his pants and shoes, he thought of what might be in store for them for the rest of the night. All he could really think about was the nighty and what it might look like, and the fact that Emma was his wife.

As soon as she came out of the bathroom, the only thing that was in his head was he was in so much trouble right now.

Chapter 11

Emma didn't have a clue how to be sexy. She knew that he was pleased with her, but she wasn't sure how to make him beg. As she made her way to him and the champagne that was sitting on the small table for her, she thought of how to walk without looking stupid.

"Christ." Pausing in mid-step, she asked him what was wrong. "Wrong? Nothing is wrong. You're amazing. Beautiful. Sexy. And mine."

"Thank you." As she put her glass to her lips, the bubbles tickled her nose and she smiled at him over the rim. "I thought you'd be naked or at least ready for me. I guess you just don't want to please me very much. Poor Kenton. Are you not in the mood?"

"Oh baby, I'm very ready for you." When he moved his hand down his incredibly sexy chest to his cock, she moaned. Glass still in hand, she reached out with the other hand and cupped him gently in her fingers. He rocked into her palm, and Emma felt her pussy soak through her tiny panties. "What do you want to do to me first?"

She nearly told him that she had no idea when a thought popped into her head. Putting the glass down on the table, her hands shaking just a little, she went to her knees in front of him. Kissing the tip of his cock through his briefs, she nearly came when he rocked into her mouth.

Peeling off his silky briefs, she licked the crown of his cock while pulling them down over his knees. They hung up there once, but she was too busy trying to take as much of him as she could into her mouth to care. When he put his hand to the back of her head, she moaned, which nearly brought him to his knees they were trembling so badly. Then he cried out for her to do it again.

He fucked her mouth, gently at first, then with more vigor. The harder he stroked the back of her throat, the more she needed of him. And when he pulled her away from him, Emma looked up at him and could see his dragon running along his skin, his eyes glazed in what she thought was pain. But she knew, in some way, that he was hurting because of what she was doing to him.

"I need you." Nodding, she reached for him again. "No. Oh baby, if you keep that up I'm going to come down the back of your throat and not in your pussy."

"You can do both." He growled low, sending vibrations all the way through her. Taking his cock back to her mouth, she swallowed him down passed the tight rings at the back of her throat. He cried out again, this time shouting that he was coming.

The taste of him was hot, spicy, and slightly sweet. As she held him, his cock filling her throat with each of his hard pounding strokes, Emma reached down between her thighs and touched her clit. That was all it took for her to come, screaming around his cock as her release took her.

He jerked from her, leaving her feeling like there was more but not sure how to get it. When he told her to stand up, she wasn't sure what he was saying really. His voice was dark and full of sex.

Before she could guess what he was going to do, she was up off the floor and bent over the bed. His cock filled her fully, his hands holding her at her hips while he pounded her pussy hard. Each time she thought she was going to come from it, the pleasure that he was giving her, she held out, knowing that when he came deep inside of her as her husband, it was going to be different than it had been before. He leaned over her, his body nearly bent half over hers, and she cried out when he cupped her breast and pinched hard on her nipple. Emma saw stars even as her body detonated around his.

Her breathing stopped; her head felt like it spun around. When her vision blurred out, then snapped into place again, she screamed. Her climax felt as if it was coming from something yet unknown to her and filling her entire being. As she came again, her body bowled over with it, Emma held onto the bed. She knew that she was set to fly away if she came one more time like that.

As Emma tried to get her breathing back under control and her heart rate back to normal, he pulled her up and turned her in his arms. As soon as he lifted her up, Emma knew that he was far from finished with her.

"This is lovely, but I need all of you." The pretty nighty was in ribbons of silk on the floor. He took her breast in his mouth. As soon as the bed touched her back, Emma wrapped her legs around his hips and held on. He entered her hard, taking her breath away once again, making screaming, much less talking, impossible.

"Come for me, baby." She nodded, knowing that she was as close as she'd ever been without going over the edge. And when he lifted her ass up, cupped her in his big hand and pulled her tighter to him, Emma felt her entire body respond.

There was no breath in her body to scream. Her heart stopped beating, and every part of her shut down for a full second. This time she was sure that he was set on killing her. Then when she came, it seemed to release a part of her that she'd never felt before. It was deep within her heart, and she knew that it would forever belong to no one but Kenton.

When she opened her eyes, she looked around the dark room. There was a small light coming from under the bathroom door, but she knew that no one was in there. Kenton wrapped his body tighter around hers, and she relished in his love.

"You killed me, I think. Is this heaven?" He laughed and kissed her on the shoulder. "It was different this time. You feel it too?"

"Yes, I did. I have never...it was as if I was having sex for the first time. I mean, sex with the right person. You are the perfect person for me." He kissed her shoulder again, then held her tighter. She knew that something had happened and really didn't want to ask.

"What do you know? And please, don't keep things from me. It frightens me to think you might be trying to keep me safe when I need to know. Okay?" He said that he would, he promised. "No secrets between us ever. As soon as you know something, I want to know. Then when I'm told something, I'll keep you informed as well. We can't make this work if we don't talk about things."

"Jorden just told me that your mom is at this hotel. She checked in an hour ago." Emma rolled to her back and looked up at Kenton as he continued. "She's alone and making several calls out of the city. He's tracking them now. He's watching Steward too. They think he's on his way here to meet up with her. They're playing right into our hands."

"What does Jorden think she's doing? And he's being careful, isn't he? I don't want anyone hurt with this. What time is it anyway? I mean, it's really late, right?" Kenton told her it was well after midnight. "So, she's calling to have us a special wedding gift delivered? What is it you're not telling me again?"

"I was working up to it. I just didn't want to ruin your sexual buzz just yet. Your grandfather called too." Emma sat up and pulled the sheet up over her nudity. Kenton just smiled at her before he looked at her face. "She's hired a hitman. He's to take you out before you get into the courthouse, and then me. We're both going to be dead by nine-thirty this morning. Not a very fitting gift now that you think about it, is it, love?"

"That's not funny." He told her that he didn't think it was either, and was trying to ease things up a bit. "I'm sorry. I'm so sick of this shit. So what did my grandfather say? That he was helping her pay them off?"

"No, he said that he's taking care of the hitman for you, that we shouldn't worry." Emma didn't want to know what that meant, and Kenton seemed to understand. "You should also know that he's taken precautions with my family as well. There are trusted guards on all of them while they sleep. Lewis said he ordered a pizza and when it came, the man at his door asked to look at it. He said he offered him a slice and the guy came in and enjoyed it with him. But he never put his gun down."

She tried to wrap her head around the fact that her mother wanted her dead, as well as the rest of the McCades. What the hell had she ever done to her? Not to mention, where did she get off trying to kill Kenton and his family? They hadn't done anything at all to her. She started to lay back down when she thought of something.

"She won't be home." He nodded. "I mean, she's not there now, at my dad's house. You said she was here in this hotel. We need to go there now and take it back from her."

Kenton only stared at her for a few seconds before he got up and started to dress. A bag for each of them had been delivered before they had gotten here, and Emma got up to do the same. Dressing and thinking had it take her longer than she thought it should have. When Kenton sat on the edge of the bed, he told her that Jorden and Grady were going to meet them there.

"Dalton is going to stay here. He said he can legally keep an eye on her and her comings and goings, but he really can't go to the house unless you want him to file a report on it. If anyone asks, he said he was going to say that she's under suspicion of fraud. Which I guess she is." She asked him what his brothers thought of what they were doing. "Lewis is jealous that he didn't think of it. Dalton said you'd make a great cop, and Jorden said that he knew you were smarter than me. Which I said you were, and he laughed at me. Grady and Vance said that you were much too smart for me and that I should simply give up on trying and let them have a go at being your husband. I assured both of them that you'd kill them the first time you slept with them, that you nearly did me."

"You did not." He turned and grinned at her. "You jerk. Whatever will they think of me now? Like I'm some sort of sex pot or something?"

"You are." He stood up and came around the bed at her. "You're not dressed yet. If we hurry, I can take you to your bed at the house and make love to you before the shit hits the fan here."

Kenton was joking, she knew that, but she reached for him. When he held her, pulling her body to his, things seemed to flow around her but not touch her as badly this time. Fear and love didn't necessarily cancel each other out, but they did make them feel less overwhelming for a moment or two.

"I'm afraid." Kenton told her that he had her and that he was never going to let her go, not ever. "While we're there, maybe we can see if we can open the safe Douglas said was there. And see what we want to do with the place."

"All right. And Vance suggested that we have someone come out and change the locks on the house. Grady has some of his shifter buddies going out now to make sure that when we arrive, we're all alone." Emma thanked him. "They love you, you know that, right? My brothers and my mom, they'd do anything to keep you safe."

"I love them as well." She laid her head on Kenton's chest and listened to his heart beating. Dragon, too, was there, the heat of him seeming to lull her into some kind of comfort she'd not had before. Looking up at Kenton, she told him that she would love him forever.

As they left the hotel, she thought of her mother. She was in some serious shit right now, and Emma hoped she got a front row seat to it all.

~~~

Anderson wanted to look her best. Her story, why she was just showing up, the best she'd ever heard, was ready and she was sure that no one was going to have a dry eye in the place when she told it. By the time that she was going to tell the world where she'd been and why, her daughter was going to be dead, along with her lover and his entire family. Sadly, they were moving in front of the line of fire and were killed needlessly. Even her daddy was going to be caught up in the cross-fire. All in one smooth move, she thought.

"You look beautiful." Anderson turned and smiled at Steward. He was going to be dead soon too. He'd become a liability to her in that she wasn't into sharing her wealth with anyone. Then there was the added fact that she'd found herself another lover, one that took his time with her first and had a dick worth having slammed up in her. Just as soon as they entered the courthouse, Steward was going to die. His body, dead and bleeding, would be the first of many that would be running on the news tonight. "People are going to wonder how you have a daughter as old as Emma."

"I have good genes." They both laughed. "You made sure that Daddy knew about the wedding today too, right? I bet he's loading his guns up right now, ready to kill them all. It's really too bad that he won't get to use them the way he wants. I'm hoping that I get to see him one more time before he dies, just to tell him what a fool he's been."

"I made sure he knew about it, anyway. He has as many people working for him as I do, if not a little more. Also, you should try really hard to not smile like you know something before we get there. Remember, you're going there to claim your inheritance now that your evil bastard of a husband is finally dead and you no longer have to be in hiding." Anderson nodded. "And try not to look too terribly pleased when your daughter is killed. It won't play well with the press. I think you should carry a box of tissues with you. That way if you feel the need to gloat, you can hide it with one of them."

"I know that. And I have a lovely hanky that I had specially made for this dress and the one that I'm going to go to their funeral in. It's beautiful, and I almost hate wearing it to that sort of thing." Anderson had it all planned out. It had taken her hours of practicing in front of her mirror to get the right expression down. And falling too. To faint with class was something that she thought she had perfected. "You know to say you knew nothing about any of this, right? You didn't say anything to anyone, did you?"

"No. Just to Baldwin about the wedding. And I made sure that there was a paper trail of me telling him. I know that all my files and shit drove him crazy, but a man has to have his tracks covered in the event that things go south fast. Baldwin didn't seem all that excited to have not just the date but the exact time that he could go in and avenge your death. But he has it." She had heard that before. Her father seemed to be distracted, Steward had told her. Anderson was sure he was just getting old and had told him to forget it. But apparently he had not. She wanted to point it out again but he started talking again. "I looked for your father's will while I was there the last time. Either he mislaid it again or he's put it in his files. I didn't have time to look there before he came into the office. I thought for sure that he'd left the house, and nearly didn't know what to say when he asked me what I was doing."

"We need to find that will so I can make sure that he didn't change it. You have been most unhelpful in that department. But he wouldn't have changed it, I know that. My father thinks he is going to live forever." He'd told her that often enough when she'd been living at home. That he'd made a pact with the devil and was never going to leave this earth until he had every penny he could lay his hands on. "The only reason he made a will in the first place was because I made him. I even wrote out all the things that he was to leave me when he passed. He'd never get it right. The man was forever forgetting to put the lid on the juice container in the refrigerator. Daddy is the most absent-minded person I know."

Laughing to herself, Anderson knew that every word out of her mouth just now was a lie. Her father was the sharpest man she had ever known. He knew where things were when she moved them without his knowledge, and would remember names of people that he'd worked with decades ago. But he loved her. And in that, he would never want to change his will to even think that his little girl was gone. It was what she was counting on.

"His limo is picking him up in an hour. The ceremony begins ten minutes before he gets there. I'm timing it so that he makes a grand entrance and a final death scene all in one. I'm going to be standing outside the courthouse steps waiting on him too."

Anderson tried not to be excited about the death of the two men in her life, and was almost afraid to speak for fear of giving it away. Instead of speaking, Anderson sort of half listened as Steward gave her a rundown of his plans.

Her passport was ready to go with her new name. There were two credit cards with her name on them as well, and as soon as the money was deposited in her new identity's account, she was going to go on a shopping spree that would last a week. After that, if she wanted to, she was going to have her new house outfitted the way she had always dreamed of, and then she'd find her a rich old man to marry and drain him dry as well. Maryanne Cantrell was going to be one of the wealthiest women in the world when Anderson was finished with her. And she'd be the hit of every party around. Maryanne was going to be making up for all the shit that Anderson hadn't been able to do while she'd been in hiding.

"Do you know what the holdup is on Bartholomew's money? I thought by now someone would have said something about it." Steward said he was still looking for the lawyer on that one. The one that her husband had used for other things said he'd never been involved in that part of Bartholomew's personal life. "Well, the sooner we get that settled the faster we can get out of town when this is done. Emma hasn't been told anything either, as far as I know. I asked her about it just yesterday morning, and even though she was only half answering me, she did say that as far as she knew the will had not been settled yet. She said that she'd let me know when she knew something important."

Her daughter. Anderson had never really liked being a mother. And especially one to Emma. She looked a great deal like Anderson, but also bore a striking resemblance to Bartholomew. Emma was also more beautiful than Anderson had ever been or would ever be. It was another reason she had to go.

Bart, she knew, wasn't Bartholomew's. She'd take that bit of information to her grave. The man she'd been having an affair with had been a pretty good lover, but he'd been stupid and had pissed her off. Killing him in a fit of rage had been dumb on her part, but there were no witnesses to his demise, and Bartholomew had raised Bart as his own. Which was good for all those around. She wondered for a moment how much he would have gotten had he lived, and smiled at the thought of how much dear Bart had missed out on.

"I guess I should have tried harder to find the will while he was alive. I mean, for all we know, the safe could hold a new will that leaves you nothing." Anderson asked him why he'd say something like that to her today of all days. "You ever find the combination? If you had looked harder and not been practicing your grief, we might have a better idea what he bought the thing for. As it stands right now, you have this enormous steel trap in your home, and for all you know, it could hold the whereabouts of everybody you ever killed."

Anderson didn't say anything. She wanted to pull a gun and blow Steward's fucking head off, but bit her lip to keep from screaming at him. It was getting harder and harder by the minute to be around this man. She was glad that today was going to be the last.

She went to put on her shoes and realized that she'd not brought them. This would simply not do, she thought.

"I don't know why it matters," Steward told her when she said she had the wrong shoes. "Just wear those. They're black. They'll go with everything. Do you really think that anyone is going to be looking at your feet right now?"

"I will not wear black shoes with a blue dress. What is wrong with you? Do you not realize how much time I've gone into with this outfit? It says beautiful without being too over stated. My shoes complete it. Now run to the house and get them. The blue ones." He stared at her, and she thought that his quick death wasn't going to be enough. "Well, what are you waiting for? We are running short on time for you to be foolishly standing there."

"They're just shoes, Anderson. Any picture that might be taken of you at the crime scene is going to be in black and white anyway, not one person is going to say, 'Holy shit, Martha. Look at the woman. She didn't even have the *decency to put on the right colored shoes for this murder and mayhem.'* Get real. No one cares." Nodding, she bit harder on her lip and wondered if there was any way she'd bite through it before someone noticed how pissed she was. "I'm not going for them. If you want them, then go get them, but I have to be in front of the courthouse when your dad gets there. If not, who will lead him into the building and into the aim of the gunman? You do what you need to, but I have a job to do."

He had a point. But she wasn't going to wear the black shoes. Anderson had an image in her head that the newspapers were going to have, and being dressed sloppily wasn't going to make it. As soon as he left her, Anderson slipped on the black shoes, hoping no one would notice what she'd been reduced to, and went to the lobby. She might not be able to make it home, but there were plenty of places she could shop for shoes.

The store was busy, which pissed Anderson off. She knew that she was being unreasonable, but she had places to go right now and this woman who was monopolizing all the clerk's time was only getting new shoes for church, which was still a couple of days away. Finally, having had enough, she asked the clerk if he could find her the shoe she wanted in her size.

"I can. Just as soon as I'm finished with Mrs. Clark here." He grinned at the older woman as he continued. "I'm the only one here, but I'm getting things done, don't you think, my dear? If you'd like to have a seat over there, I'll be with you in a minute or two."

"No, I don't want to have a seat over there. I want waited on. I've been here for over ten minutes already and I have things to do." The man looked at the clock over the counter, then back at her. "I don't care how long you think

I've been here. I can tell time, and I know for a fact that I've been here ten minutes. Now, do you have this shoe in my size or not?"

Mrs. Clark, smart woman that she was, told little Ted to go ahead and wait on her. But he only shook his head and told the elderly woman that he was going to find her a shoe that she liked. Anderson picked up a shoe with full intentions of bashing him over the head with it when someone touched the back of her head.

"Move and it will be all finished." Nodding, she moved back when the man pulled her. "You have two options...well, one really. The other is more like a result. Death if you don't pick well." Anderson started to turn around and ask him if this was a joke when her daughter walked in. Emma told the man that she had it now. The gun, because Anderson had no doubt that was what it had been, was suddenly gone. She looked at Emma and tried to smile at her.

"I don't know what that was all about. I just came in here for a pair of blue shoes." Anderson looked around and realized two things at once: they were alone in the store, and Emma wasn't where she should have been, at her own wedding and murder. "I thought you were getting married today. I mean, I heard that today was the big day for you. I was just here seeing about getting some shoes for my dress. For your wedding."

Anderson snapped her mouth closed. She was talking stupidly and hated that. Not having a clue what else to say, Anderson looked around the store for something to point out, anything to bring the attention away from her and her babbling when Emma answered her question.

"Why would you think that I'm getting married today?" Anderson had no clue. She wasn't sure at this point if Emma had ever mentioned her marriage before, or if Steward had told her. Anderson was sort of lost as to how to continue. "I know about the shoes, by the way. We've had your room monitored since just after you checked in. Steward, by the way, is not going to meet my grandfather at the court house, for he's not going to be there either. And the gunman you hired to kill me? He's been arrested as well. The McCade family, my family, they're all safe."

Anderson tried to think. Laughing a little, she wanted to sit down and think her way out of this. But Emma was there now, and she had no idea what was going on. When Emma sat down Anderson wanted to run, but the ding of the little bell over the door had her looking in that direction, and she saw Kenton standing there.

"I guess I was misinformed, about everything. I was going to surprise you by showing up and seeing my only daughter getting married. I don't know why you'd think I would want to know why there...why my father hired a hitman for you, but I really don't care for your tone." Emma said nothing, and that made Anderson nervous again. "I guess I'll be going then."

"No, you won't." Anderson looked at the door and wondered if she could rush the big man there. But when Emma laughed, she looked at her again. "He wants you to try. To get by him, that is. Kenton wants you to try to get out of here so he can kill you now. I have suggested that you're not that stupid, but I'm beginning to wonder. Are you, Anderson? That stupid, I mean?"

"Don't call me by my first name, damn it. And what right do you have to keep me here? I am your mother, Emma, and I expect you to straighten up and act right. I don't know what you're talking about with that hitman and Steward—other than he worked for my father. The nerve of some people. If you don't mind, I'm leaving." When Emma didn't say anything, she moved to the door. But before she could get to it, the man there—Kenton—changed into a large dragon, complete with sharp scales down his long back and tail.

Anderson fell back on her ass and stared at him. This could not be happening. She knew about shifters, of course, but this man was a dragon—*a fucking dragon!*—and he was standing right over her.

"Kenton said to tell you to stay right where you are or he'll burn you alive. I'd do it if I were you. He's not in the best of humor where you're concerned. We have a few hundred questions for you, and you're going to answer them for me." Anderson didn't even move her leg, which was cramping up. "Grandda is on his way here too. He wants to have a long conversation with you before you're arrested as well. He's not happy with you either. I mean, what sort of sick fuck orders their perfume after they're dead and charges it to their dad's account?"

"I couldn't very well go back to the house and get mine, now could I? Besides, it's none of your business what I did or didn't do. You'll be dead soon enough anyway. And what do you think I'm going to be arrested for, Emma? For being alive? No one is going to care when they find out why I'm here now." Anderson thought she'd ask her why not, but she only stared at her. "I've had to run because your father was so abusive to me. It was pretend I was dead or I would be. He was a monster. I mean, he even knew where you were all that time, and he left you there to be abused by your own brother."

"Is that why you didn't tell me? And so you know, Bartholomew knew that Bart wasn't his son. He wasn't very happy about that either. He felt for some reason that you weren't worth even mentioning in his new will. I had a peek at it, so you know. That man hated you very much for what you did to him." Anderson looked at her father as he stood there speaking to her. The big dragon didn't bother him, but she had a feeling that if she moved, he'd do just what he said he would. "You didn't come to me and tell me that Bartholomew was hurting you…why is that? You came to me about every other little thing. Nor did you tell me that he was abusive to you when you were supposed to be dead. Yet you lived in a house that he paid for. He kept you well dressed, warm, and happy. I don't believe that abusive part any more than I believe you to be a loving, wonderful daughter. What changed in you, Anderson? What changed you into such a bitch?"

"I'm still your little girl, and Daddy, I'm so glad that you're here. You have no idea how he treated me. I was so afraid of him. And he forbade me to go to you. I tried, let me tell you." She tried to move, but the dragon moved closer to her and she had to still again. "Can you make him go away, Daddy? He's frightening me. I just want to hug you, but he's keeping me from you."

"So you can put the knife deeper in my back? Or did you think to pick my pocket while you were at it? I have nothing for you, Anderson. Not one thing." Anderson wanted to ask him about his will but was actually afraid of the answer. "You are dead, so there will be nothing once I'm gone either."

That got her attention. He had changed his will, or if he hadn't already, he would soon. She sat up, no longer thinking about the dragon but of what this was going to cost her if he cut her out now.

"You can't do that to me. I have plans for that money." Her dad said nothing as he sat down next to Emma. "I suppose you're leaving it all to her. Well, I'll have you know that she's not going to get any of that either. I've taken care of things."

"You mean the men you hired to kill the McCade family? Did you really think that I'd not hear about it? That the men that you contacted wouldn't have come to me when they heard what you were doing?" Anderson asked him who had told on her. "Does it matter? And then the icing on the cake was hiring someone to take me out too. That really hurts, Anderson."

"I didn't mean for you to be killed, Daddy. You know that." He only sat there, and she sat up as well. "You have to believe me when I tell you it was all Steward's fault. He forced me into this."

"Yes, I just bet he did. So you know, he said the same thing about you just before he was killed. The amount of senseless murders nowadays is amazing, don't you think? Or perhaps, like you, he'll come back someday. I'd not count on that, but you never know." She wasn't sure of the tone, but at least he wasn't telling her that Emma was going to get it all. "I'm going to let the cops come in and take you now. I've seen and heard all I want from you. More so really than I wanted, but I had to have closure as well. I do hope that once they have you behind bars you'll be able to see the error of your ways."

"Daddy? You can't do this to me. I need you. I'm your little girl. If you leave me here with all this hanging over me, I'm going to go to jail. You know that they won't treat me right there. I need you to save me." As soon as he stood up, she did as well. And as she leapt on his back to drag him down, she tried to tell him he had to listen to her. It never registered that he'd used the gun that appeared in his hand on her until the loud pop sounded and the pain took her breath away. "Daddy? Did you just shoot me? Did you...Daddy?"

Chapter 12

Kenton stared at the file in front of him. He knew on some level that he should be writing something in it, but for the life of him all he could think about was Emma and what she was doing right now. The house, her father's house, needed to be finalized, and she was doing it alone. The way she wanted, but still, she was alone.

"You could go help her, you know." If Jorden had been sitting there all along, he'd not noticed until just then. "I know that she said she wanted to do this alone, but you could just close up and go to help her. I would."

"She pretty much kicked me out when I stopped by there on my way in here this morning. She said that she had some demons to get rid of and she didn't want me there. She really hates it when I see her cry. I hate it, too, because it tears me up inside. But she said she needed to do this." He'd been hurt and had called his mom, who told him to behave himself. That none of them knew what the poor girl was going through. "Mom said that she needed this time to do this, too. She thinks Emma has been holding on to her sorrow for too long and needs to get this done or explode."

"Did you ever open the safe?" Kenton nodded. "Anything important in it, or just a big box that he ordered?"

"Bartholomew thought it was funny on some level that Anderson would see it and not be able to open it. He even hinted to the fact that she'd never guess the code, even though she should have. The code was simply one through four. That's it, just simply the first four numbers. But he left Emma jewelry and cash in it too. Things that he said that she should have that the government didn't get a part of. Taxes, he thought, were the ruination of the world. There were books too. First editions that he had bought in the hopes of giving them to her for her birthday. I think, in a sad way, he knew that his days were numbered even without the cancer being a big factor. He just didn't trust Anderson at all." Jorden said it was a hard life, living the way these men did. "Yes, I agree with you there. He also left her the deeds to several pieces of property that he owned. Several of which you've been trying to buy up for a few years, as a matter of fact."

"Really? That's nice. Do you think she will sell them to me?" Kenton shook his head. "Oh well. I guess I can ask her if she can rent it to me for a while. Is one of them the one on Basher Street? You know, I've always thought that place would be perfect for my studio and place to live."

"It is. Emma said the same thing when I mentioned that you coveted that place. And she and I talked it over, and she and I are giving you the building." Jorden started to tell him no, but Kenton raised his hand up. "She will sell you her father's home if you want it. Cheap. I think that's why she's there today. She needs to put that part of her life away for good. In fact, that was one of the reasons she wanted to get it done today, so that I could talk to you about taking it off her hands. You will, won't you?"

"It's a big house." Kenton nodded. "What am I going to do with a house that big? I can barely fill the apartment I have now with stuff. And even if it is cheap, which you say, I'm not a rich doctor like you are. My money is more…feast or famine kind of income."

Kenton knew for a fact that the reason his brother had never filled his apartment of five years was because he wanted the building on Basher and was saving all his money. The one time it had come on the market, when Bartholomew had purchased it, as it turned out, it had gone for well over three million dollars. Then nothing more had been done to it. Jorden's plan was to offer the current owner, someone none of them knew at the time, more than he'd paid for it, and Jorden had been saving for that day.

"She said that you can have a harem in it if you wish." Jorden only smiled at him. "There are three other houses that her grandfather owned, and two more that her father left her. She's going to give each of you a home. And if none of you want them, then she'll sell them off to the lowest bidder. She wants to finish it off. You need to do this for her. She wants you to have the house and the building. She said that she owes you."

"All I did was hold her back when the police tried to arrest her grandfather. She would have been most upset if they'd arrested her too." Kenton nodded. "Did you ever think that Baldwin would only get a slap on the wrist for killing Anderson? I mean, it was self-defense and all, but fuck man, he killed his own child. You think that had anything to do with his untimely death?"

Her grandfather had died in his sleep a week after the funeral of Anderson. Kenton thought the man had been poisoned, or at the very least had poisoned himself. But he was gone now, and because Emma was his only living relative, she had inherited his wealth as well as that of her father. Along with a list of places that he'd stashed money in the event he had to run, he'd also left Emma the keys to several safety deposit boxes that were also filled with old coins and other relics that had a receipt attached to each one of them. The man had been busy in the last days of his life. Kenton's wife was the wealthiest woman in the world right now, according to most newspapers, and it seemed to matter as little to her as it did to him. Kenton thought Emma was the most broken too. This had been terribly hard on her.

"About the houses...I'll think about them both. I want them, but I don't know what I'd do with them either." Kenton said nothing. Jorden would take them if for no other reason than Emma would bully him into it. "I have a big show coming up in a two months. Are you still going to be able to get away to go with me?"

"I am. I've been looking forward to this as much as you have." Kenton leaned back in his chair, shoving the file away for another time. "You've really made a name for yourself. I'm really proud of you."

Emma wasn't going to go with them on this trip. This was just him and his brothers, as it had been in the past. She was going to spend time with his mom and a project that the two of them were cooking up. He had a feeling that it was literally that, cooking. Emma was the best cook he'd ever seen, and she loved it more than any other chef he'd met. She was making her famous pumpkin pecan cobbler for them for dinner tonight, as a matter of fact.

The trip was going to be epic this year, Kenton knew. Every year, at one of Jorden's shows, the six of them would get together and have a blast, spending the entire time flirting and getting drunk and eating some of the best local food they could find. This time was no different, other than it was in Paris and not here in the States, and Kenton's flirting days were over.

As he knew he would, Jorden waved him off about the compliment. When he stood up, Kenton took a moment to look down at the file in front of him and nearly laughed as he, too, stood to leave the offices. It was his last patient for a while. He and Emma left in a few days for their honeymoon. They were setting sail on a month-long cruise, and that was another reason she wanted to settle up the wills from her family. He had a few surprises for her there too. Kenton liked being a romantic, as Emma was fond of calling him.

They were just turning to go out the door when Jorden turned to him with a grin. "Okay, I'll take the house and the Basher building. I don't know what the asking price is on the house, but I'll take it." Kenton nodded and made a mental note to remember to tell his mom she owed him ten bucks. She said he'd never go for it, and Kenton said he would. "What is the asking price?"

"Before I answer that, what sort of change do you have in your pocket?" Jorden said nothing and reached into his pocket and showed him the sixty-seven cents he'd had in his pocket, along with a drawing of some woman on a napkin and a rubber band. "That's the asking price. Congratulations, you own a home."

"You can't be serious. Less than a buck and you're selling me two places that I've wanted for ten years? You guys can't do that." Kenton told him they were and that they neither one needed the money, so that was how they'd decided to sell them. "But she's going to have to pay taxes on it. I mean, inheritance taxes are a bitch."

"They are, but no. All the houses were in her name before their deaths. I don't know how they managed that, but she owned them before each man passed away. Her father explained it as he'd owed her so much more than he could leave her, and Baldwin just did it. He'd hired a new attorney too, just before he left to see us that day that Anderson died." Jorden asked him if he was upset over the way that Emma was giving away the houses. "No, we talked it over, and she asked me what I thought about giving them to you. I told her that you wouldn't just take it and neither would the others. She'd have to sell it to you or you'd turn her down. No matter how much you wanted it. But she'll be thrilled that you are taking it. Do you want the furniture that she leaves behind too?"

"I don't have any more change." Kenton laughed and told him that they had no use for six more houses of furniture. "Yes. Whatever I don't want, I'll let her know. She can...I don't know, donate it, I guess. Or sell it. I understand that her dad collected antiques like most men do women. Is she going to open a shop up? That might be the perfect way to get rid of a lot of this stuff too."

"Yes, the house is full of them. Her old bedroom had been converted into a holding room. I think there were several hundred paintings in there when we did a walkthrough. Most of those have receipts on them so that she wouldn't be accused of stealing them. The ones that didn't have been put into storage until such time as they can figure it out. But she's donated a large portion of those to the local library to hang on the wall. She said that even small towns need a little culture." Jorden asked if he could look them over. "Yes. She said that whatever you want, just let her know. They're yours too. Oh, and I'm supposed to ask you about a piece that she saw on the brochure that you had printed. The large vase that has a dragon on the front of it. Are you selling it at the next art show?"

"It's hers, tell her. When I made it, I hadn't met her, but then when it was fired, I knew she was going to get it. Tell her that...tell her that she needs to remember each time she sees it that she is our dragon queen. Your wife, she's very generous. I would say stupid if it were anyone but her, but why is she doing this for us?" Kenton could have told him that she wanted them to have everything, but he doubted that his brother would believe him. "Is it because she loves us?"

"It is. Most of it anyway." Kenton opened his car door but didn't bother getting in yet. He wanted to talk to Jorden more, needed to, he thought. Jorden would listen, he knew, and not judge. Kenton wondered what he'd say if he told him the real reason that Emma was doing this, and knew that he could trust his brother to not make fun of her. "What if I told you that she was doing it so you'd love her? That she has it in her head that to give you this means that you might really love her?"

Jorden paused in mid-step and asked him if he was serious. Kenton assured him that he was. His brother looked angry at first. Then he laughed. Kenton had to smile; Jorden had a very infectious laugh.

"Does she have any idea how much...well, I guess she doesn't or she'd not do this. You do know that we all love her like a sister, right? And that any and all of us would die for her? Hell, I'd die for both of you if necessary." Kenton told him that was the point. "I don't understand."

"She wants you to love her like she's your friend. Having brotherly love, like the one she had before, hasn't gotten her very far. I don't even think she's sure how to love a brother. Not like you guys anyway. Emma thinks that with her background, and the way things have turned out about her family, that you guys are going to think I got the short end of the stick and that you only tolerate her because of me." Jorden asked what he meant. "Her brother, as you know, was a fucking piece of shit. Her mother lied about her death and tried to kill her. Her grandfather had ties with some very scary people, and her dad was a loan shark, and not in the nicest sort of way. She has never had anyone other than me to love her for what she is. You guys, she loves you very much, but she has no idea how to show you. I think this is her way of telling you how much you mean to her."

"I see. So we should take the houses and keep our mouths shut? That is, if we want to keep her happy and to show that we love her? You know that's just stupid. We all do love her." Kenton told him that would be a start, and that it wasn't him that had to be convinced. "You're right. Because as of right now, I'm going to make sure she never doubts how much she means to me. Not for the rest of her life."

"Good for you." Kenton put his arm around his brother's shoulder and told him that he did truly love him as well.

"I love you too, old man. And you can buy me dinner. I know for a fact that Emma is having dinner with her new mother-in-law—namely our mom—and we should go and save her. Also, if we save her, maybe she'll let us all have some of her cobbler when we get back. Maybe if I asked her nicely, she'll make me some more of those macaroons too. Christ, a man could die happily eating those until he went into a coma." Kenton knew that she had already baked him the cookies and that they were right now in the kitchen of his apartment. "Really, we should go and have dinner with the rest of the family. I'll contact them while you drive. It'll be fun."

"You should taste her chocolate chip ones. Or the strawberry fest, she calls it. I'm telling you, I'm going to have to join a gym soon if she keeps cooking like she is. But in answer to your question, the rest of the family is already meeting at the new restaurant in town, and you're the guest of honor. And since you got your new house so cheap, you could pick up the check." They were still laughing as they got into his car.

Kenton loved his family very much and could not wait for them to find their other halves. Because there was little doubt in his mind that they were coming, and soon. According to Dragon, the next one was on her way now.

~~~

Jasmine watched the bidding on the box of what she could only determine was junk. But as she'd learned over the last few years, one person's junk was another one's treasure. Her own business thrived on that. When the man lifted up the next three boxes, she made her way to the other end of the table to wait for the bidding to be over. The lot that she was interested in was next.

Things had turned out so different than she'd wanted for her life. Her marriage had failed big time. Her ex-husband had left her pregnant and alone for the most part. Even before the ink had been dried on the paperwork he was staying with them less and less, only coming into their lives when he wanted something or needed a place to flop. So just a few months ago, just before it all went to shit, she's filed divorce papers. But by then she'd lost her home, her car, and any savings that she'd had after that just trying to keep their head above water. Jasmine hated more than anything that she'd ended up drowning no matter what she'd done.

Then her grannie had gotten sick too. And even before Jasmine and her son could move in to help her out, some large corporation had come in and bought up the condo she was living in, and they were all out on their asses again. It had been a real struggle for them for a while, and still was some months, but they were together and that was what was important.

As she stood there thinking about her lot in life, she was bumped from behind hard enough to shift the several glass pieces in front of her. The auctioneer glanced her way and winked, but didn't pause in what he was saying, the gibberish that only people in this business ever understood.

Jasmine didn't like the big auction houses. Nor did she care for the house auctions that were all neatly boxed up and put on the lawn in order of whatever the auctioneer thought of as sets. Books all together, records all in a line with the stereos and radios found throughout the house. Some of them even went so far as to make the beds up they were selling, as if someone gave a crap about how neat it was.

She liked this kind. Where the company running the auction would go in, empty out the drawers or table tops, and dump it all willy-nilly in a box or two. Then when they took it outside, they put it there and moved to find another box to set out. She got some of her best deals at those types of sales.

She moved closer to the table when the bidding stopped on the boxes. It was time. Her lot was up. There were several pieces in the one box that she wanted, and nothing more than some office supplies in the other two.

Things she might be able to use, but she really wanted to get the box that held the jewelry. Jasmine was willing to go up to ten dollars a box to get them too. She looked around to see the competition.

There had been a man who had been looking at the same boxes when she'd first arrived to this part of the yard, but he had wandered off about ten minutes ago. That sometimes happened when there were two rings going. She hoped that he stayed away until she got what she wanted, knowing that he'd be the one to drive the price up to more than she was willing to go. When she knew there were two rings going to happen, Grannie would come with her and bid on the items in the other tent or part of the yard to help out. Today she wished Grannie could have come too.

Jasmine didn't care for the stranger for some reason. It's not that he'd done anything to her or even spoken to her, but there was something about him that made her feel dirty. He looked...sketchy, as her grannie would have said. Looking around as the auctioneer started out the bidding at fifty dollars, she didn't see him and was relieved. When no one bid on the boxes even when he came down to ten bucks, the auctioneer asked for a starting point.

She waited just long enough for no one to bid before she did anything. It was her plan to get him as low as she could before he started moving up again. Jasmine looked like she wasn't sure and put up her two fingers to start the bidding. She knew that it was going to be a war and wanted to show she was ready.

Four minutes later, she nearly leapt for joy when she got all three boxes for six bucks. No one, it seemed, wanted them but her, and she was tickled pink about it. Picking them up, turning down the help of the elderly man next to her, Jasmine made her way to her truck. It was days like this she was happy to have learned a thing or two from her grannie. And not just about bidding and antiques either. It was about life in general.

"Trust no one. Give no one the time of day, and never make eye contact." Sort of scary, Jasmine knew, but it had saved her a lot of grief since she'd been flipping her purchases she got at auctions. She'd just opened up the doors on her truck and had the safe inside open when she heard the voice behind her. Jasmine tried to ignore him, but he spoke again.

"Hello? Excuse me, I'd like to make you a deal on those boxes." Jasmine didn't move to turn toward him but slipped the few pieces of gold and the pretty earrings she'd fallen in love with in the safe under the floorboard of her truck. "I was going to bid on them, but I seemed to have gotten tied up on the other side of the yard when something.... Never mind. I'd like to offer you double what you paid for them."

Double? Not nearly enough, and even if it was, she wasn't going to take it. She wanted them and had been there to get them. It was just his bad luck, she supposed.

"No thanks." She turned to him then and was taken aback by his size. The man had to be over seven feet tall. He was big too, muscled like he lifted up buildings in his spare time. "I'm sorry that you missed out, but I won them fairly."

He nodded and smiled, which was neither reassuring nor friendly to her. He told her that was fine and asked her if she was from around here. Instead of answering him, she shut her door and locked it and moved away from him and her truck. His voiced carried over the crowded field when he made her another offer.

"I'll give you a hundred bucks a box for them. That's more than you can make flipping that stuff, if that's what you have planned. As I said, I was tied up and really wanted to try and get them for someone else." Too bad. It was a lot more than she was going to get, but she never stopped moving. "Two hundred for each box. And I'll even help you get that dresser you bought in your truck."

Jasmine stopped and turned to stare at him. Two hundred bucks a box? He wanted something in those boxes. And for some reason she thought it was the beautiful earrings. She had no idea of their worth. They could have been diamonds and sapphires for all she knew, but she doubted that. Or nothing more than rocks someone found in their driveway and polished up.

Jasmine turned to look at him. It also scared her that he'd been paying enough attention to her to know that she'd gotten a dresser earlier today. But she also knew that he was offering her too much money for her to turn it down. Not that she still wanted to sell to him, but if she didn't, Jasmine had a feeling that he'd take it from her and she'd be out of her money, even as little as it might have cost her.

"I only want one thing out of them. Would you be willing to let me have it?" She already had taken out what she wanted and was planning to donate most of the rest to the local charity drive to use in the upcoming yard sale. "If that's okay, I'll take the six hundred for them. I'd be stupid to turn that down."

"Depends on what it is." She nodded and made her way back to her truck. Her heart was pounding now and she was actually afraid to open her door. She wasn't that far from other cars and people, but would they come and help her if this man decided to hurt her? And what if he'd seen where she'd hidden the other things she'd bought? Opening the door all the way, she handed out the three boxes she's just put in and reached in blindly and took out the first thing her fingers touched. The ugly costume jewelry was one of the things that she was going to donate. "Yeah, you can have that. I have no use for jewelry like that."

He took out his wallet and she tried not to notice the gun that was tucked tightly against his ribs. She was sure that he'd not meant for her to see it, but now that she had, Jasmine couldn't unsee it. He handed her six hundred dollars and asked her if she was ready to put the dresser in the truck. It took her befuddled mind a moment to wonder what the fuck he was talking about.

"Yes, that would be great." It took them less than ten minutes to get the big heavy dresser in her truck. As she was putting her dolly in with it, he wandered off and she leaned against her truck, shaking. Whatever that man was, she wanted no part of him. Looking around, she decided that whatever else she wanted wasn't worth it and started for her truck. But a small voice, low and sort of masculine, told her that she needed to stay for a little while longer. That it was unsafe for her to leave when he did.

Closing her eyes, Jasmine knew she was more stressed than she'd thought over the incident. But she did move to the bigger tent to see if the other items on her list were still up for bidding. To her way of thinking, she had extra money to use now, and decided to try a little harder for the pretty pie safe that she already had a buyer for.

It was nearly three hours later when she left. The pie safe was tied up with her dresser, and she had several more boxes of stuff to add to her online store. She'd even managed to get herself a headboard that would look nice in her room, as well as some things for Gavin. As she was pulling out into traffic, she thought again of the man.

"I'm not sure what he wanted, but I have a feeling that he's not going to find it now." The voice in her head, the one that had been talking to her off and on all day, told her she was right. "Yeah, and what makes you so sure? I mean, you did know that that woman was going to only go to seventy-five dollars, but what about the man? And why are you even talking to me? Or even for that matter, why am I listening to you?"

He will mean you harm when he finds out what has happened. If he lives. Jasmine knew that was right for some reason, but didn't ask how the voice in her head would know that. And when he came looking for her, this man who overpaid her, she'd be ready for him. Jasmine was not like other women. She wasn't the least bit helpless. *No, you are not.*

Deciding that she really did need to get out more, Jasmine ignored the voice telling her that she needed to pack up and leave as soon as possible, that it was no longer safe for them. It was their home—hers, Grannie's, and her son's—even if it was a shack that was cold in the winter and hotter than hell in the summer. She worked and lived there, and it was home.

It took her longer to get home than she'd hoped. Stopping to fill up the tank and her own belly had delayed her. But she wasn't going to stop at a hotel, as had been her plan when she'd left home early this morning. She wanted to see her family, small as it was. When she saw the welcoming light over the front porch, Jasmine felt as if all the stress of the day melted away.

Pulling her truck into the big barn, she got in the back seat and pulled up the carpet and opened the large safe.

The modification had been done by her and Grannie a while back, and she was glad for it. It was their safety net, a place that even without going to auctions, held things that they could use in an emergency. There was several thousand dollars in cash, her grannie's records, as well as Gavin's birth certificate, and a gun. The gun had come in handy a couple of times in the last few years.

They had cut a hole in the floorboard, then put in a large steel box. After welding it in, making sure that it was flat even with the lid closed, Jasmine put the carpet back, then covered the entire thing with a floor mat. Unless you got up under the truck to look, no one would ever know that she had the safe there. And that was the way that she wanted it.

Even though she'd never been robbed at an auction, Jasmine and her grannie had decided there was no point in tempting fate. They found that having just the extra security kept them from feeling defenseless too. They didn't really buy that many things that required a safe, but when they did, it went right in there as soon as it was bought.

"You get your things?" Smiling, Jasmine turned and nodded at her grannie. She was standing in the doorway in her long gown and a ratty robe. "Gavin is in his room. Don't think he's sleeping. Waitin' up for you, I think. He's done his homework too, so you know. Never even had to ask him about it. Told me that he'd done it on the bus again."

"I'll go and see him. The teacher said he was doing really well, so I'm not worried that he's not doing it." She pulled out the earrings and other things and showed them to Grannie. "I found these in a box and couldn't resist them. Aren't they lovely? And I got them really cheap too. Then this man came along and bought the rest of the stuff for a good price too."

Jasmine had already decided to downplay the thing with the man. Not that she thought Grannie would get mad at her, but she might tell her that she'd been a fool. Because the more she thought about it, the more of an idiot she thought she'd been. There were so many clues about her that he could have gotten if he wanted to find her. Her license plate, for one thing.

"I guess if you like just plain things. Just some old costume stuff, but if you like them that's fine with me." Grannie looked at the pie safe. "That for Mrs. Dunlap? She's gonna love it. Better shape than the pictures, I think."

Jasmine looked at the earrings. She supposed one would call them a cuff for the ear. But plain? Costume jewelry? She didn't think so. They were gorgeous. She held one up to the light and watched as the sparkle of the blue stone in the dragon's mouth danced around the big barn.

The tail of the dragon would hang from the front of her lobe. It was long and detailed, and she thought that it was made of silver. The rest of him, his body would wrap around her ear with his hands holding on to look as if he were perched there. His head and the big blue stone in his mouth would hang over the top so that it looked as if he was climbing up her ear and looking down at her. His wings were closed, but she could almost see them in flight when he left her ear. They'd be as blue as the stone in his mouth and brilliantly light against the sky. Jasmine smiled at her fanciful notions. She wasn't one to go on about things like this and thought it was funny that she'd done it over a pair of earrings, of all things.

"You should wear them. They're pretty, I guess, for a girl, so you should put them in." Jasmine was sitting on her son's bed about ten minutes later, and he didn't seem to think the earrings were all that special either. "You bought them 'cause you liked them. Wear them, Mom. You know that you wanna."

Gavin was her most prized possession. He was the only thing that she was glad for from her marriage to David, his father. At eight, almost nine, he kept her sane. Most of the time, Jasmine had to remember that he was just a little boy to refrain from telling him her deepest secrets and fears. Some of those even scared her. He'd been through a lot, her little man, and she hoped every day that she was doing the right things for him.

Nodding, she got up and went to his bathroom and pulled out the alcohol to clean them with. She was actually shaking she was so excited. It occurred to her that the voice in her head had been telling her for the last hour she should put them in as well, but like she'd done since she'd been home, Jasmine had ignored him. After they were cleaned up the best she could, Jasmine put the first one in. The tingle of something ran down her spine to her toes.

"That was weird." Gavin asked her what. "I'm not sure. I guess the house settled a little and I felt it on my feet." A lie, yes, but she didn't want him to think his poor old mom had gone off the deep end. She was sure he'd thought that when she'd left his dad.

Gavin got up and got her a mirror so she could see them, and the tingle seemed to move over her entire body again. Not painfully, but just to let her know that something was there. As she cleaned the other earring, she thought perhaps this was a bad idea and wanted to pull it out and sell them. But Gavin told her that she was pretty and Jasmine didn't want to disappoint him, not even in this.

Laughing just a little, she let Gavin help her put the other one in. As soon as he clipped the body of the dragon to his tail through her ear, Jasmine felt a screaming in her head that made her sick to her stomach. Then the pain in her entire body made everything blink out for a second. And that was when she saw him, the big man that was suddenly a dragon. He just changed, like he had been one all along. Holding onto the sheets, she tried to think what to say when Gavin told her that her nose was bleeding.

Her thought was that the dragon had come to take her, which was silly. What dragon? And where would he have fit in her body? But she knew, as surely as she was sitting there with a tissue on her nose, that something was wrong.

There is nothing wrong, my lady. You have brought another part of me to life. She started to ask him what he was talking about when she realized that she was talking to the voice again. *I am here. The dragon in the jewelry. I can tell now that the part that you have awakened is my wings. I shall be able to fly high in the sky when the other parts of me are brought to them.*

"Them who?" She looked at Gavin and realized she'd spoken aloud. Telling him she was fine and that he had to go to bed now, Jasmine tucked him in and told him she loved him. If she was going to go nuts, she wanted Gavin to know that she loved him. Going to her room, Jasmine leaned against the door and closed her eyes.

You must take me to my owner now. He will be most pleased to have you as part of his life. Jasmine decided that the voice in her head was from too much stress. And tomorrow she was going to make a day just for herself. *That is a wonderful plan. You will need to go soon after, however. The McCades are awaiting you.*

"I don't know what you're talking about. I don't know any McCades, and I'm certainly not going to be a part of any of their lives." She realized that she was talking to him again, herself she supposed. "Leave me alone. I don't want you talking to me again."

But I must tell you how to get to them. You will love them as much as I do. I have told Emma about young Gavin. She is happy about that. Jasmine started to tell him not to tell people about her son, but that would just be stupid. *You are not stupid. Why do you keep saying that?"*

"Because I'm having a conversation with a voice in my head and not wanting him to tell fake people about my son. I think that borders to being about as nutty as the Christmas log that Grannie makes every year." Jasmine hated that thing too. It was too sweet and salty, a combination that had never set well with her. "I'm going to contact Mrs. Dunlap tomorrow, let her know that I have her pie safe, and then go and have my hair cut. I might even have a nice lunch in a restaurant with cloth napkins that are set on the table and not in a venting box."

I'm afraid that I don't understand. She didn't bother explaining it to herself either. *No matter. You will be all right once you have made your way to them. I wonder which dragon you will be paired with.*

Dragon. She thought of the dragon she'd seen, the one that was a man too. And whatever was going on with him, Jasmine wasn't going to have any part of it. And she was selling the earrings too. Even for a dime if she had to.

Before You Go...

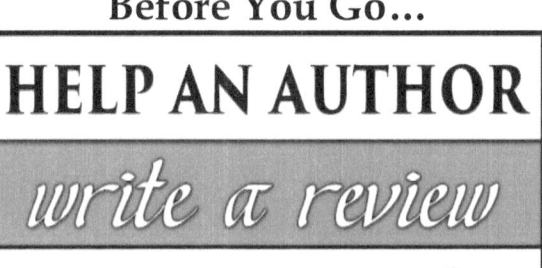

Share your voice and help guide other readers to these wonderful books. Even if it's only a line or two your reviews help readers discover the author's books so they can continue creating stories that you'll love. Login to your favorite retailer and leave a review. Thank you.

KATHI S. BARTON

Kathi Barton, author of the bestselling series Force of Nature, lives in Nashport, Ohio with her husband Paul. In addition to writing full time Kathi likes to spend time with her eight grandkids, three children and three children-in-laws. She writes to relax and have fun.

Her muse, a cross between Jimmy Stewart and Hugh Jackman brings them to life for her readers in a way that has them coming back time and again for more. Her favorite genre is paranormal romance with a great deal of spice. You can visit Kathi on line and drop her an email if you'd like. She loves hearing from her fans. aaronskiss@gmail.com.

Follow Kathi on her blog:
http://kathisbartonauthor.blogspot.com/

www.ingramcontent.com/pod-product-compliance
Lightning Source LLC
Chambersburg PA
CBHW021958190626
46808CB00017B/2225